EVE DEVON

I write sexy heroes, sassy heroines & happy ever afters...Growing up in locations like Botswana and Venezuela gave me quite the taste for adventure and my love for romances began when my mother shoved one into my hands in a desperate attempt to keep me quiet during TV coverage of the Wimbledon tennis finals!

When I wasn't consuming books by the bucketload, I could be found pretending to be a damsel in distress or running around solving mysteries and writing down my adventures. As a teenager, I wrote countless episodes of TV detective dramas so the hero and heroine would end up together every week. As an adult, I worked in a library to conveniently continue consuming books by the bucket load, until realising I was destined to write contemporary romance and romantic suspense myself.

I live in leafy Surrey in the UK, a book-devouring, slightly melodramatic, romance-writing sassy heroine with my very own sexy hero husband!

You can visit my website at www.EveDevon.com/ and follow me on Twitter @EveDevon.

The Love List

EVE DEVON

HarperImpulse an imprint of
HarperCollins*Publishers* Ltd
77–85 Fulham Palace Road
Hammersmith, London W6 8JB

www.harpercollins.co.uk

A Paperback Original 2014

First published in Great Britain in ebook format by HarperImpulse 2014

A catalogue record for this book is
available from the British Library

ISBN: 9780008114923

This novel is entirely a work of fiction.
The names, characters and incidents portrayed in it are
the work of the author's imagination. Any resemblance to
actual persons, living or dead, events or localities is
entirely coincidental.

Automatically produced by Atomik ePublisher from Easypress

For Rachel—my fellow Chiari ZipperHead Club member, because you understand not only what it is to be creative, but to be courageous too.

Chapter One

'What the..?' Nora King strung together a stream of amazingly coherent swear words for so early in the morning as she flapped her hand around in a wide circle, trying in vain to dislodge the shoe she had just managed to superglue to her hand. This was so not happening.

'Okay. It's okay. Breathe,' she instructed with an edge of panic when it became apparent she was going to do herself a serious injury if she continued to wang her arm about so insanely.

She counted to ten.

Then, calmly and without any sense of drama, lest the shoe somehow suspected she was going to try and wrench it free again, she placed her free hand on top of the harbinger of doom and pulled. Gently at first, then harder, as tears of frustration pooled at the outer rims of her eyes.

'Damn it, budge, why don't you?' Desperate, she glanced around the private bathroom that connected to her office, looking for something to prise it off with. This was what she got for trying to be clever and fix her beloved shoes; the ones with the magical confidence-boosting properties, on the morning of her eight a.m. breakfast meeting with Eleanor Moorfield—designer of the shoe now attached to her hand—instead of the night before, where it had been clearly scheduled on her To Do list. But last night, after getting in late from a day of meetings, followed by an uncomfortable visit with her sister, Sephy, she had bypassed the shoe-fixing in favour of a large glass of red and some sleep.

'A-hah,' she exclaimed in a light-bulb moment. One-handed she upended the contents of her bag and rummaged for a nail file. Locating one and holding it aloft triumphantly, she smiled at her genius in the mirror, before trying to slide the file between the sole of the stiletto and the palm of her hand.

No deal.

A trickle of hysteria bubbled its way to the surface.

It was now one hour and fifteen minutes before she was due to deliver the pitch of her life. She'd been working on the presentation for six weeks. Six weeks of silly hours. Six weeks of devising, developing, practising and polishing. She had it on super-secret authority that Eleanor Moorfield, ex-model turned award-winning shoe designer, was looking to relocate her headquarters from Italy back to England. The Moorfield brand was right up there with Louboutin, Jimmy Choo, and all the other 'have to have' shoes women salivated over. Securing a contract to provide business premises for the Moorfield headquarters, shop units and manufacturing set-up would be a real coup for the King Property Corporation. Not to mention prove to herself that she hadn't lost her touch. That she still had what it took to get out there and get the business in.

On her own. Without help.

KPC had been, and always would be, her life.

By the time her father had retired and she'd stepped up as CEO, KPC had over three hundred commercial buildings it owned and leased out and Nora's first challenge had been to secure the company's future against an economic downturn. Confidence had come from her passion for KPC, her unwavering dedication, and the knowledge that she could always get guidance from her father if needed.

But when her father suffered a major health crisis she'd been forced to approach her brother Jared in New York, and persuade him to return to the family he hadn't been part of for ten years and the company he had declined to run—the company she loved, for help.

She had always known her brother's expertise was on loan and ever since Jared had returned to his own life in New York, she had been working to implement the changes he had helped come up with. Changes that would add to KPC's portfolio of property services and ensure the family-run company would recover from its dip and go from strength to strength.

Her confidence had taken a battering, though.

So get the Moorfield contract and hopefully she'd stop second-guessing every decision she made since the death of her father seven months ago and then Jared's return to New York. Get the contract and she'd have so much work she wouldn't have *time* to second-guess every decision she made.

She wanted desperately to land the account. For herself. For her father. Okay, mostly for her father. For the faith he had placed in her.

Blowing a strand of straight black hair out of her eyes she swung back to face herself in the bathroom mirror. It had all been going so well. All she'd had left to do was go through the pitch one last time before quickly repairing the spot where the sole had parted from the leather upper on her shoe. Nora sniffed dejectedly. Possibly she shouldn't have been wearing this pair so much lately, but they made her feel so in control and can-do when she had them on, and today, especially, she'd wanted to show she loved the Moorfield brand. That she owned the vintage editions as well as the latest designs. She should have stuck with the perfectly service-able but non-Moorfield stilettos she was wearing, or concentrated on doing one thing at a time, like any other normal professional.

Oh, a sudden brainwave had her rushing towards the door back into her office. Opening it she looked left and then right. What for, she wasn't quite sure, but with perspective now dangling precariously, it felt like the right thing to do. Then, dashing across her office, stopping briefly to grab the large tote bag she had used to transport some of her files that morning, she encased her 'predicament' inside the bag, dragged the straps over her shoulder, and fought one-handed to set free some of her trapped hair.

Finally composed, she wished with all her might that salvation was about to take the form of her assistant Fern, who, if luck was on her side, would turn out to secretly be some sort of shoe surgeon.

Pushing open the door to the reception area, which housed Fern's desk, she squeaked, 'Fern? Two words: Help, Emergency,' and then came to an abrupt halt as she spied a tall, gorgeous—if she was absolutely forced to form a fleeting impression—man, dressed in jeans and a charcoal-grey duffel coat, standing beside Fern's desk. 'Oh.'

Okay. This was most definitely not her five-foot-and-half-an-inch assistant, Fern. This was a well over six foot tall *tree* of a man, making five-foot-ten-inch Nora feel unexpectedly petite as she hovered uncertainly in her office doorway.

'Technically that's three words,' claimed the man, turning from where he'd been staring at a portrait of her father to look over at her.

'Three words?' Nora blinked. She didn't have time for a maths lesson. She needed help. She needed a miracle. She needed…a knight in shining armour strong enough to separate her shoe from her hand? Not that she could afford to be fussy. If the hand had to come too, so be it.

'Mmmn. "Oh" being the third,' he explained, shoving his hands casually into his coat pockets.

Somehow, despite a warm smile that induced a quite unneces-sary, in her humble opinion, heart-skipping-a-beat moment, Nora felt sure actual knights didn't come equipped with a mean streak in pedantry. She went to finger-quote and realised she couldn't. Pushing the straps of the oversized carrier bag over her shoulder, nerves jangling on their very last nerve, she rose to the bait.

4

'*Technically*, who are you, the Word-Count Police?'

No reaction. Well, if you discounted the slow sexy amused lift to his grin. Which, she decided, she really must.

Was this the famous boyfriend, then? Maybe he'd dropped Fern off and was waiting around to say goodbye when she came back from wherever it was she was. She looked around and finding the reception area empty, realised that Fern was probably getting the coffees in. She thought about her usual vanilla latte and, with hand clamped to her shoe, couldn't help thinking she was going to need something stronger.

Of its own accord, Nora's gaze swung back to Mr Office Imposter. He was definitely noteworthy. If you went for the whole twinkly blue-eyed, full wide smile, chiselled and stubbled jawline look, with the dirty blond slightly overlong hair in a ruffled style that made a woman itch to muss with it further and thus stake her claim. Nora couldn't help herself; she ran her gaze from head to toe. He certainly had the whole broad-at-the-shoulder, lean-at-the-hip thing going for him.

Yeah, had to be the boyfriend. Shorter women always ended up with really tall men, who looked like they could pick them up and put them right where they wanted them.

Lucky Fern.

Nora felt kind of bad; Fern worked all hours of the day for her, which didn't leave her much time to meet up with Mr Gorgeous, here. She wasn't sure she could be so forgiving if the roles were reversed.

She shook her head slightly. Maybe she'd accidentally inhaled the glue while performing the spectacularly stupid stunt of sticking her favourite shoe to her hand, because it definitely wasn't every day she was struck down by—

Nora breathed in sharply.

No way was she thinking love at first sight.

Lust at first sight, maybe.

Love at first sight was for wish lists that you wrote with your favourite coloured markers when you were ten.

Mr Office Imposter stared right back at her, knowingly allowing her to look her fill, and so, she guessed, it would be rude not to. After all, Nora liked to think she had good manners. And then there was the fact that it was *her* office he was in.

Shoe-gate was all but forgotten and seconds felt like minutes as she stood there watching him watch her. Worse, the more the laid-back confidence behind his eyes traitorously affected her breathing, the more she was struck by an insane impulse to slake her tongue over parched lips—wanting and not wanting his incredible blue eyes to track the movement.

Excruciatingly bad form, Nora. Fern had obviously got there first and besides, she definitely didn't have time to indulge in whatever this silent thing was that they had going because none of this was getting her where she needed to be, in shoe-stuck-to-hand-less land.

Hugging the bag protectively to her chest, she tried to find her way back to the idea that she was a professional businesswoman. 'I'm Nora King,' she said, introducing herself.

'Ethan Love. I—'

'Hey, I see you two found each other,' Fern said, as she breezed in with the requisite cardboard tray of hot drinks. 'Sorry I wasn't here to do the formal introduction, but when I couldn't find you,' she added, looking at Nora, 'I assumed you'd gone on the coffee run. I thought I'd catch you up by taking the lift, but you must have got back first.' Fern whizzed over to her desk to set down her purse and the tray. Casting Ethan a brief look, she said, 'Nora has a little thing about waiting for the lift and usually takes the stairs.'

Nora felt heat creep up her neck to tinge her cheekbones. 'Er, that's your boss you're labelling as pernickety and impatient. Not sure your boyfriend and I know each other well enough for you to divulge all my endearing qualities.'

'My boyfriend?' Fern looked from Ethan to Fern with a funny look on her face. 'Holy crap. You haven't done the introduction thing?'

'Of course I have. He's Ethan Love. Your boyfriend.'

'He is Ethan Love. He is not my boyfriend. He's Daisy's uncle.'

Nora felt a spike of something that might have been relief that he wasn't Fern's boyfriend before confusion set in. 'Daisy who?'

'Daisy, your niece,' Fern said, speaking extra slowly and looking at her as if she had left her brain somewhere.

'Don't be ridiculous. Jared is Daisy's uncle.'

'Jared King is your brother, right?' Ethan said patiently. 'Well, my brother is Ryan Love…your sister Sephy's ex and Daisy's dad.'

'No, Daisy's dad is called—' *Love-Rat.* At least that was what Nora had privately labelled him when he'd run out on her sister. She managed to stop herself from saying the words out loud. Ethan Love…Ryan Love. The dots got closer together until they joined up. Wow. But why was his brother here? Nora tried to process his presence and suddenly could only think it must have been something huge to have brought Ethan Love to visit. 'Oh no, please tell me your brother isn't—' She couldn't bring herself to say the words. She might not have ever understood the bad-boy draw of her sister's ex and she might have been pleased when he'd upped and moved away so that her sister didn't have to see him around town doing a very passable Peter Pan impression while managing only haphazard interest in his daughter, but Nora didn't want her sister to go through another bereavement.

'I'm sorry,' Ethan was quick to reassure. 'I should have thought about what it would look like dropping by so unexpectedly. I simply need your help to run something past your sister.'

Nora stared at Ethan. Why did she get the feeling that this wasn't going to be simple? With a sinking heart she really didn't see how she could possibly juggle one more thing, but if this had something to do with her sister—if her sister needed her help, she would find a way.

Plan A, to meet with Eleanor Moorfield minus her shoe appendage slipped out of the window and sloped off into the distance, where, the way her day was going, it would undoubtedly be joined by Plan B and Plan C.

'Would you like me to reschedule your 8 a.m. for later today?' Fern asked, looking at Nora with concern.

'I can wait until your meeting is finished,' Ethan said, mildly. 'I just got off a plane so I could do with checking in to a hotel and sleeping. I only stopped here first to make an appointment. I'm afraid I didn't realise how early it was.'

Nora was so busy wondering how he'd managed to charm security into letting him through to her offices that she only caught the tail end of Fern's repeated offer to reschedule her breakfast meeting with Eleanor. Hand clenching within the confines of the bag, she said, 'Thanks, Fern, but you'd better cancel it altogether. Something else has come up, which means I couldn't have made it today, anyway.'

'Something else? Since when? You were so pumped for the meeting. You're ready. The pitch is ready.' Fern glanced down at Nora's feet. 'Wait. Those aren't *the shoes*. Where are *the shoes*? Don't tell me you forgot to bring them in with you. Not you, The Shoe Princess.'

Nora felt Ethan's gaze drop to the four-inch black stilettos she was wearing before slowly moving up the length of her legs to the hem of her black pencil skirt and then up further, across her cream jacket before finally coming to rest on her face. Fern and Nora knew each other, warts and all, but somehow with Ethan standing there, taking everything in, it was really hard not to feel exposed. And warm. Very, very warm. 'I can be interested in shoes without being a "princess" about it,' she said, trying unsuccessfully not to pout.

'Right, so what's with the shoe bag?'

Nora glanced guiltily down at the bag clutched across her midriff. It had the name of a well-known Italian boot-maker emblazoned across the front. Of all the ironies... Nora felt her grip on reality slipping as she admitted, 'Actually, I do kind of need your help.' She blew out a breath. There, that hadn't been so very difficult. Doing her best to ignore Fern's snort of incredulity, she rushed on, 'Yes, this is really me, really asking for help, which you can tease me for later, but right now I need you to help me come up with a Plan B—a suitable excuse for postponing my 8 a.m. with,' Nora looked at the wall clock and blanched, 'with only one hour's notice.'

'Just for the hell of it, what happened to Plan A?' Ethan interjected, pulling out one of the chairs in front of Fern's desk and obviously settling himself in for the duration.

'Forget Plan A. I am so beyond Plan A it's not even funny,' she answered, a tad more irritably than was perhaps wise, given that it was she who was asking for help and not the other way around.

The heartbeat-altering grin made an appearance. Ethan seemed to find her waspishness more amusing than insulting. He probably never found himself in embarrassing situations.

Taking another deep breath, Nora focused solely on Fern. 'The problem is, I can't do my pitch today, on account of a little accident, which doesn't need a whole Q and A,' she insisted as Fern stepped forward with a frown on her face, 'I'm absolutely fine—I simply…need to cancel. And come up with a suitable excuse. I mean I know fact is stranger than fiction,' when Nora heard her voice rising alarmingly she began pacing, to try and outdistance herself from her own stupidity, 'but in this case fact sucks. Fact turns me into a laughing stock and I can't afford that—'

'Is she always this hyper?' Ethan asked Fern, as if she wasn't there.

'No way. Only when she's done something…oh, good grief, Leonora, have you been multi-tasking again?'

'Only a little bit,' Nora shot out defensively, before squeezing her eyes shut in mortification, because really, who had ever heard of a CEO not being able to multi-task?

'We've talked about this. You know nerves and multi-tasking and you don't mesh. I swear, for someone so ultra-efficient in every other aspect of life, it beggars belief. What's happened and why on earth don't you put the bag down?'

Nora winced.

It seemed a show-and-tell was on the horizon.

'It is *kind* of shoe-related,' she whispered as she started lowering the bag from where her arm was hidden inside, 'it's kind of a,' she gulped and went for broke, 'help, I've super-glued my shoe to my hand, kind of a mess.'

The bag floated silently to the floor and the next thing she knew, Ethan was standing in front of her turning her hand one way and then another, as if she were some sort of interactive museum exhibit.

'How on earth..?'

'Oh, by all means, let's share.' Nora's head bobbed up and down as if she couldn't wait. What was one more ounce of mortification? 'Let's see. Well, this is one half of a pair of vintage Eleanor Moorfield shoes. On my feet, these shoes say: This woman knows what she's about. You can trust her with your business—with your life, which is why I intended to wear them today for a pitch I've been working on for weeks. Sure, I may have, technically, been supposed to fix the sole of this one yesterday. But, sometimes life gets in the way and anyway, I found some glue this morning on Fern's desk and, well, some of the glue must have seeped out while I was pressing the sole closed. By the time I had finished running over my presentation, and,' Nora's head dipped as she mumbled, 'taken a couple of work calls,' she waved her hand-shoe combo in his face, '*this*, had happened.'

'Fascinating.'

Nora's gaze shot to Ethan at the quietly mumbled word. With the heat of humiliation stinging her cheeks, she really could have done with both hands free to fan herself, or at the very least, hide behind.

'Did I mention Nora is addicted to multi-tasking?' Fern chimed in helpfully.

'There's no way I can win a business pitch like this. Doesn't exactly make for a great hand-shaking experience, does it?'

'Oh, I don't know,' Ethan said, his grin full. 'You'd get my vote for originality. My guess is he certainly wouldn't forget you.' He stroked his fingers over her hand. Heat zinged all the way up her arm and into her neck. Okay, so snatching back her hand might send a signal that she was affected by his touch, but at least it would shock her brain back into working. And, a working brain would be good. If only to stop her feeling like some silly ingénue under his gaze.

'He is a *she*,' she answered. 'And believe me…she won't be so easily charmed, especially since it's one of her designs that's attached to my hand. I'm going to reek of ineptitude. Not exactly the look I was going for.'

'Never mind all that,' Fern said. 'You should be in hospital getting that seen to.'

Hospital? Nora hadn't really done hospitals much lately. Not since her father—skidding her thoughts to a halt, she tucked her tongue between her teeth and started pacing again. There had to be another way. 'Ooh, quick. I need your computer.'

'My computer? Sure but—' Fern got out of the way in time for Nora to plonk herself down at her desk in order to slowly, single-handedly Google: How to remove superglue.

'Ha,' squinting at the screen, she clicked on several entries. 'Right. I need something containing acetone chemicals.' She scrolled down the page. 'Otherwise known as…nail-varnish remover.' She turned to Fern, who was looking over her shoulder. 'Here's the part where you tell me you never leave the house without nail-varnish remover?'

'Oh, sweetie.'

'Nooo! Come on,' Nora looked skywards, 'I asked for help and everything. Oh,' Nora sat bolt upright as a new thought occurred. 'Shops. Shops will save me.' She looked at the expression on Fern's face. 'If they were actually open, that is.' Whose bright idea had it been to have the meeting at 8 a.m. anyway? It was like some sort of weird conspiracy.

'I have to win this pitch, Fern. I have to. I can't f—' Nora broke off and hung her head as the full enormity of what she'd been about to admit hit her. The last thing she needed was to give Fern the impression she was about to crumble if she failed.

Her vision blurred as she looked down at her hand. She'd have to cancel the pitch. So be it. These things happened. Except, usually she did everything in her power to ensure that these things didn't happen. Not to her. Providing strong leadership had been what she'd been trained to do by the best in the business—her father. She hated that lately, every business move she made, had her questioning herself. When she'd heard on the grapevine that Eleanor Moorfield was thinking about returning to London, Nora had suited-up, taken the gamble and approached her directly. Now, it stung to have to admit that a little multi-tasking may have defeated her and made her look as if she wasn't quite as super-efficient and in control as she liked to appear. It was beginning to look as if she deliberately sabotaged her own success.

She breathed in sharply. She did not like the sound of that. Not one little bit.

'Why can't you ask someone else to do the pitch for you?' Ethan asked from where he was stationed the other side of her. 'You must have account managers who usually handle this sort of thing.'

'I don't want to ask any of them to handle this particular meeting for me,' Nora answered, realising the statement looked as though she couldn't delegate. Why hadn't she said something more along the lines of: she liked to lead by example or keep her hand in? Not that she needed to explain herself to him.

'Why don't I do the pitch for you?' Ethan asked.

Nora's mouth dropped open and she craned her head to look up at him as if he was insane. The raised eyebrow she got back in response suggested its owner cared not one jot what she thought of him.

'Why don't you…?' Again she flapped her hand-shoe in his face.

'Because despite all evidence to the contrary, I'm in the market of showing KPC in the best possible light at all times. I'm not about to put a complete stranger into a meeting it's taken me weeks to set up. I don't know you from Adam.'

'Hey,' Ethan held up his hands as if to ward off any histrionics. 'I rather thought you were making a case for all hands to the pumps. But go ahead. Be Miss Independent. It's working out really well for you, so far.'

Indignation battled alongside embarrassment. 'I'm sorry, I seem to have missed the part where you mentioned you were a property acquisitions lawyer, salesman or account manager or used to securing major business contracts.' She raked her gaze down to his battered trainers and back up again. 'You're not even dressed appropriately.'

'But maybe he could do it, Nora,' Fern said.

Her head whipped in the opposite direction to stare at Fern. 'You've only just met the man.'

'But, well, he's kind of family, isn't he?'

'He is *not* family. Besides, if he's anything like his brother, he'll get distracted by something pretty before he even gets to the meeting.'

In the stark silence Nora couldn't quite believe she'd been so rude. Asking for help was new enough to her. Graciously accepting it was obviously still at the conceptual stage.

The urge to run and escape was immense. A feeling that was becoming increasingly persistent of late.

'It seems to me,' Ethan said, as if her words had had no effect, 'you need someone who can represent your company without making a fool of himself, charm the client into outlining their needs and then promise you can deliver those needs within a reasonable time and for a reasonable fee. I don't see a problem. I am such a guy.'

His arrogance astonished her. But while she sat there staring at him like a stunned mullet, couldn't she actually see him charming

Eleanor Moorfield right out of her shoes?

'The idea is preposterous,' she said to counteract the vivid imagery.

'Clock's ticking,' he said patiently, testing her resolve.

'You're not even wearing a suit.'

He turned to indicate two travel bags stowed by the desk and she remembered he had said he'd come from the airport.

Her mind raced. It would take months to scout out another client the size and scope of the Moorfield brand. By then, KPC might still be surviving, but would it be flourishing under her guidance? What would she have if she didn't have KPC? Her brother Jared had his own corporation and a beautiful new fiancée. Her sister, Sephy, had a fledgling business and a darling daughter. It was up to her to keep the family company run by someone in the family. She couldn't bear the thought that she might run her father's legacy into the ground—not when she believed so much in the company and not after Jared had helped her set KPC back on track for a bright future.

She looked at Ethan. At this point, what did she have to lose? If he didn't land the account, no one within KPC would be any the wiser and she'd just work her butt off finding another lucrative contract to beef up the company's profile. If he did land the account...

No.

She shouldn't even be entertaining the idea.

But the thought of the Moorfield account slipping away...

She looked at the wall clock before her gaze settled back on Ethan. 'But why would you help?' she asked without filtering.

For the first time since she'd laid eyes upon him, his casual demeanour altered slightly and for all the caution she threw at herself, she was intrigued by the chink in this knight's armour.

'Call it family loyalty,' he said, obliquely.

Chapter Two

'So in between rescuing damsels, what is it you actually do?'

Ethan heard Nora ask the question from where she'd nervously set up camp outside her executive bathroom door. Whatever she'd taken from his reference to family loyalty had had her relenting and agreeing to show him the presentation after he got changed into a suit.

Ethan braced his hands on the marble vanity and stared hard into the bronze-toned mirror in front of him.

What was it he actually did?

Allegedly he was in the business of helping people. Whether he continued to get to do that was another matter altogether after the risk-assessment report was filed.

Turning away from the mirror, he searched his bag for his wash kit. He didn't know what all the fuss was about. He'd got the kid out, hadn't he? Like any other member of the team would have left him there if there'd been even the remotest chance of getting him out. He hadn't placed anyone else in danger. Surely the important thing was that Pietro was alive and hopefully back with his family by now—not whether going into that building had been reckless and against protocol.

Ethan turned back to the mirror and ran a hand over his day-old stubble, realising he didn't have time for a shave anyway.

God, he was tired. The insomnia was getting really bad. But he'd deal with it. No need to make it complicated. No need to dwell.

Angling his head toward the door he went with the job he hoped he would still have after the report was submitted, rather than the job title stamped on his passport. 'I work for a charity that organises disaster relief. I go to whichever disaster zone I'm deployed to and help provide shelter, water, food, etc.'

Silence.

He wished he could see her reaction. He was willing to bet she was standing on the other side of the door with a sexy little 'v' etched into her un-Botoxed forehead, her tempting mouth dropping open slightly in shock.

'And you've come back recently?' she asked.

'Via a quick stopover to see my brother, yes.'

'Where is it you've been?'

Ethan blew out a breath. 'Northern Italy.'

'Where the earthquake was?'

'Yeah.' Ethan deliberately kept his eyes open to stop the memories flashing before his eyes.

'So…you have a really important job, then?'

'If you want to think so,' he said lightly. He smiled, imagining it might be a little hard to reconcile what she'd just heard alongside her previous judgement of him.

'So…the Love Rat must have done something really bad to necessitate you coming home and then here.'

Huh. Clever.

His smile turned wry. He supposed he couldn't really complain about the Love Rat tag she'd used for Ryan. It was quite the accurate description of the brother he had known before Ethan had deliberately started working so hard; he hadn't had time to keep up regular contact.

He wasn't going to hide from telling Nora where Ryan was. It was why he was here. But right now he had an opportunity placed before him that meant he didn't have to think about the situation he'd left behind in northern Italy or about how seeing his brother really made him feel. Right now he wanted to do something he knew he could do, and do well. And if it helped burn off the latent energy so that maybe at some point later today he'd be able to sleep, even better.

Probably after he got some sleep things would go back to feeling simple and he'd stop worrying that his boss was going to judge him negatively for something any decent person would have done.

Realising he'd left his other bag behind, he called out, 'Can you pop through to reception and pick up my garment bag, take out the blue suit and bring it to me?'

'What did your last slave die of?'

Ethan looked in the mirror, liking how her harrumphed tone put the twinkle back in his eyes. 'Happiness when I came out of the bathroom naked to fetch my own clothes?'

As he started removing jacket, top and jeans, he tried to make out more dark mutterings from the other side of the door before it was opened a notch and his clothes were pushed through the tiny gap and dumped on the chair inside the door. A few seconds later the door opened a little bit wider and she mumbled, 'There was no tie in your bag.'

'Oh, yeah. Don't use them.' He had no problem meeting her curious gaze and as her eyes dropped lower to take in his chest and the ink that wrapped around his right pectoral and shoulder, his grin grew impossibly wider. 'Too restrictive.'

She shut the door firmly between them.

He chuckled. He might be suffering from insomnia, but even the fug of running on empty hadn't diminished the spark of attraction between them.

Unbuttoning the white shirt, he shucked into it.

Settling back into life after a deployment was always hard. Granted, he usually had the satisfaction of knowing he'd done a good job and all he could to help.

This time everything was different.

This time…well he wasn't willing to take that one out of the box for analysis quite yet. All he knew for certain was that for the first time in a long while he'd questioned his ability to make a situation better and he'd questioned his ability to keep doing a job he loved so much. Especially during the hours when he'd been talking to Pietro, trying to figure out how to get them both out. Shaking his head, he put the suit on and determined to think about something else.

For his brother to track him down and make contact was unusual, but when the first phone call from Ryan had come, Ethan had remained calm.

Relaxed.

Calm always got him through deployment. And relaxed had always got him through dealing with his family, and in particular, his kid brother.

He'd accepted that phone call with the deliberate laissez-faire attitude his brother was so expert at, and when Ryan had told him he was in trouble, he hadn't asked near enough questions.

Ethan was going to carry the guilt of that for a while, no matter that in his opinion his brother hadn't ever known what real trouble was. Never saw what Ethan saw every day in his work. Ryan's version of trouble could be alleviated by him simply growing up and changing his attitude.

His brother had had to call a second time before Ethan properly computed what was going on. By then, coinciding with being called into his superior's tent and told to take some leave while they filled out their report, the last thing he had been feeling as he packed his bag to take the plane home to the UK, was calm and relaxed.

Ryan needed his help. Of course Ethan would help.

Any concern over the fact that his own future hung on the outcome of a report could be relegated to second place.

He only hoped getting Sephy King on board with his idea to help his brother wasn't made more difficult by her older sister, Nora.

Nora King.

He wasn't sure what he'd expected. Not a princess in skyscraper heels with defiant fiery button-brown eyes and the dreamiest, creamiest, palest of complexions, though.

She was the living embodiment of the corporate females he deliberately avoided these days, but there was something about her that slammed right into him, leaving him a little breathless. Even with the business-as-usual façade she wore, he could see the struggle she was trying to survive underneath. How she couldn't quite hide the fact that grief had stripped her bare and she didn't know what to do about it.

He'd seen that same hollowed-out shocked look on people's faces when their worlds had exploded and they'd been left to try and rebuild what they could.

Combing his hair back from his face, he thought about the woman on the other side of the door. He really shouldn't, but damsels in distress being something of a rarity these days, he felt like indulging himself.

Probably not the wisest move; especially as the plan had been to sort things for his brother, so he was ready to go and finish the job he'd started if he got the call from the charity. *When*, he got the call from the charity. He wasn't going to waste energy thinking negatively.

Nora was standing by her uncluttered glass desk when he entered the office, her head angled towards his luggage as if trying to absorb all the information about him she could by osmosis. It occurred to him that no woman should be able to look that regal while having a shoe stuck to her hand, but Nora made it look easy. And sexy. Or maybe the insomnia was finally tipping him over the edge.

Buckling his belt he walked over to the garment bag and took out a pair of formal shoes to put on. He supposed if he was going to be back for a while he'd have to get used to being suited and booted again.

Doing this presentation for her and taking her to hospital to get her parted from her shoe would definitely help take the edge off the restlessness that came with being back.

Maybe taking her out afterwards would help keep that restlessness at bay. Especially if he took her somewhere colourful, lively, relaxed and about as far removed from the crumbling half-finished job he'd left behind him.

His gaze swept over the rigid set to her shoulders and the way she sucked on her bottom lip. On second thoughts, perhaps he'd take her somewhere quiet. Intimate. No distractions.

'I can't believe you don't have a tie with you,' she said.

'You're lucky I have the suit with me.' He usually travelled lighter, but he'd had the King's world in mind when he'd packed. If he wanted their help, he'd figured a bit of conformity would ease the way.

'I don't know why you would bring a suit but not a tie,' she continued.

Ethan smiled inwardly at the genuine suspicion in her voice. He bet Nora liked her guys bound by the formality. Traditional. Safe. *Boring.* He caught her watching him out of the corner of his eye. 'So what do you think?' he asked. 'Brush up as well as the next guy?'

Nora seemed to consider his question seriously. What? Was she actually weighing him up against every other guy? The notion had him wanting to puff out his chest and give her something a little more concrete for her to use in comparison.

Slowly she walked over to him, her fingertip tapping against her lip and everything within him stilled. He felt the air displace softly as she lifted her arm to brush a piece of lint off his shoulder.

'You'll do.'

He breathed out. 'So glad you approve,' he said, his voice deeper with her so close. 'I guarantee you Eleanor Moorfield will.' He liked that that brought her head up. Liked the spark that flared briefly in her eyes before she got herself under control. 'You want to show me this presentation, Princess?'

20

She really looked as if she didn't. Great, in the short space of time that he'd been changing had she lost confidence in him? He should have told her about his other job. 'I guess now is a good time to tell you that when I'm not volunteering for the charity I run a chain of deluxe leisure facilities.' He shoved his hands into his trouser pockets, unused to having to sell himself quite so much. 'I'm not a virgin at talking to potential clients.'

Nora regarded him silently for a few moments and mumbled an, 'Okay,' as she rounded her desk to switch on her laptop and bring up her presentation, then gestured for him to sit down and read through it.

A whole sixty seconds passed before she suddenly said, 'Wait. You're part of Love Leisure?'

'I guess you could say that I am Love Leisure. Problem?'

'No. No, of course not.'

Despite not liking that she looked more impressed by what he'd just revealed than she had sounded when he'd told her about being a disaster-response team member, he still found himself wanting to alleviate any doubt. Love Leisure's success was paramount in providing enough income so that he could volunteer as a rapid-response team member on pretty much a full-time basis and as it was his name above each of the branch doors, he intended to keep it successful. 'I have good people in place so that the business runs like clockwork while I'm away, but I do keep my hand in when I'm back. You don't need to worry. I can do this.' He returned his attention to reading through the entire pitch, nearly getting to the end before the nervous foot-tapping beside him became too pronounced.

'This is fine. I can work with this.'

'Hang on. If it's only fine—'

'Relax,' he reassured when the foot-tapping started going into triple-time. 'You give good presentation.' He loved the way she blushed. He exited the PowerPoint presentation and logged into a business-networking site so that he could search the designer's profile. 'So where are you meeting this Eleanor Moorfield?' he asked.

'The Savoy. She has a suite.' Nora glanced at her watch. 'We can talk some more about KPC on the way.'

'You're not walking in those?' Ethan said, pointing incredulously to her feet.

Nora glanced down at her shoes. 'What's wrong with these?'

'They're not a little difficult to walk in?'

'I am a woman, Ethan. I can walk in any shoe you put in front of me.'

'Okay, let me put it another way: have you actually seen what the weather is like outside? You'll ruin them before you get halfway there. We'll take my rental. What are you doing?' he asked as Nora reached across the desk for her phone.

'Calling Eleanor's assistant to tell her it won't be me doing the presentation.'

'Don't do that. Don't give her any opportunity to cancel. She won't mind if I show up in your place. Trust me.'

Nora looked at him as if he'd used the dirtiest two words in the English language. He caught the glimmer of something at the back of her eyes and wondered whether she was actually going to let him do this for her. 'Come on,' he said picking up the laptop before she had time to think. 'We can go over everything in the car.' As she followed mutely alongside him, he wondered if it was him she didn't trust, or herself. Except, she was CEO of a company that had been going for decades. You didn't rise to that position without being good at what you did. Well, you could rise to that position, he thought, glancing once again at the portrait of her father as they headed out, but you couldn't keep that position. Not if you weren't good.

By the time they pulled up outside the Savoy, Nora was looking pale and pensive. Ethan went through the presentation highlights again. It didn't seem to help. If anything, she looked as if she was about to pass out.

'You don't look nervous,' she accused. 'Why don't you look nervous?'

'What is there to be nervous about? This will be a cinch.' He shot her his most disarming smile.

'And there was me thinking that nerves helped a person perform better.'

'Interesting, but I've never had any complaints about my performance.' He tried not to laugh as her eyes transformed into huge saucers. 'Look, I'm good at thinking on my feet. I promise not to give the company secrets away and I won't sign anything put before me. I'm going to go in now.'

Nora glanced at the valet patiently waiting to take the car. 'Where shall I wait for you?'

'How about the Starbucks across the street? When you see the car being brought around, you'll know I've finished.'

'Okay. Good. That's good.'

Ethan released his seatbelt and was about to open the car door when he felt Nora's hand, or rather, her shoe, on his forearm. 'Ethan, thanks. I realise it may not look like it, but I really do take KPC incredibly seriously.'

'No problem.' He opened the car door and scooped up the laptop. He nodded towards a hotel doorman to open the passenger door for Nora and walked confidently towards the hotel's entrance.

Forty minutes later he was getting into the car, impressed with the speed with which Nora had managed to sprint across the road in the shoes she was wearing, to be at his side.

'Well?' she queried.

'How about we get in first,' he said.

'So get in already,' Nora answered, jogging around to her side of the car to pull open the car door and slide in gracefully, which amazed him all over again, considering she still had a large bag covering her arm.

She waited a nanosecond for him to pull out into the traffic. 'Well?'

'It was interesting. I think it went well.'

'You only think? Damn it. I knew it. Cancelling *would* have been better. What was I thinking, letting some complete stranger take over? I mean just because I've heard of Love Leisure, it's not remotely the same industry as property services.'

'Little joke.' He smiled as he heard her inhale. Turning his head to briefly look at her, he said, 'Relax, it went well.'

'Oh.' The confidence in his voice seemed to appease her a little. 'What's in the goodie-bag?' she asked, craning her head to the back seat, where he had placed the large glossy, burgundy, signature Moorfield bag.

'Something that tells me I know the meeting went well.'

She remained silent, but against the hum of the car's motor he could practically hear her brain chugging away, trying to decide between staying polite and demanding to know what went on with Eleanor Moorfield.

'So what happens now?' she finally asked.

'Now we wait.'

'Oh.' There was a lengthy pause and then he felt her turn her head towards him. 'In case you haven't worked it out already, I'm not that good at the whole waiting thing.'

Ethan stopped at the traffic lights and turned his head, grinning from ear to ear and feeling invigorated. 'I'm sure I can come up with a way to pass the time.'

'I have to tell you,' Ethan told Nora as he eased the car out of the hospital grounds an hour later and headed back into traffic to drop Nora off at her office. 'Your definition of a debriefing and my definition of a debriefing differ considerably.'

Bad jokes and double entendres aside, Nora was still having trouble believing how deftly he'd organised someone to see her in the casualty department after insisting on waiting for her. He'd taken one look at how quiet and uncomfortable she'd become the closer they got to the hospital and, once more, assumed the knight-in-shining-armour title. A couple of those artfully aimed sexy smiles of his and she'd bypassed triage and was being ushered into a cubicle for treatment.

'Maybe I'll have to check out your version, one day.' Oh, she did not just say that! If the chemicals they'd put on her hand to melt the glue had tongue-loosening properties, oughtn't they to warn a patient about that?

Ethan flashed her a hot, private smile and Nora tried to concentrate on breathing evenly. She really had to stop this now. This flirting thing she had going with him. Now would be a good time to remember that flirting, and everything that usually came after, was off her To Do list for the foreseeable. She didn't have the time. Couldn't afford the distraction. Look what happened to her when she tried to multi-task.

Admittedly it had been a while since she'd indulged in more than flirting. Her eyes squeezed shut as she remembered Sephy's comment from last night—that if she wasn't careful, outside of a work context, she'd forget how to talk to men altogether. Coming on top of the rest of the lecture she'd received from her younger sister, the comment had stung. Nora sighed. As if Sephy hadn't known that accusing her of being a workaholic, who'd put her grief on hold, wasn't going to put her in the best of listening moods. She knew Sephy's little digs were designed to sneak under her shield and penetrate, but after the disaster of her last relationship Nora knew that relationships weren't for her. She had much clearer goals. Until she was back on an even keel at KPC, work came first, second and third for her.

'How's the hand?' Ethan asked.

His question had her turning her attention to his own hands as they rested competently on the steering wheel. Any idea of work flew straight out the window as she wondered idly how those hands might feel against her skin, smoothing their way up and over her naked flesh, from hipbone to breast.

Nora blinked, squirmed against her seat and looked down at

the bag, now containing the remnants of her shoe.

'Okay,' she said, determined to shake off the attraction she felt for him. Peering closely at the hand in question, she cleared her throat and forced some more words out. 'No lasting damage. It was a close-run thing, but thanks to the wonders of modern medicine, well, chemicals, actually… Turns out I probably could have done it DIY with the nail varnish remover.' She sighed dramatically as she opened the bag carrying the rest of the shoe she had embarrassingly asked to keep because it was vintage Moorfield. 'To be honest, I think I'm experiencing a little separation anxiety.'

Ethan's deep laugh trickled over already hyper-sensitised nerve endings and left her feeling as though someone had left a window ajar in her heart. She had a desperate need to keep busy. To be doing many things at once. Anything to stop her nerves jangling at the idea of what a kick it was to make this man laugh. Honestly, the sooner she was out of his car and breathing in some normal, heavily polluted, air, the better it would be for her sanity.

Now that she didn't have to worry about missing out on pitching to Eleanor, Ethan's scent was staging a staggering assault on her senses, causing her to behave completely out of character. It was time to rein herself back in, she thought, as she suddenly realised whereabouts they were. 'Oh, this leads straight to the back entrance of KPC's offices. It's about a hundred yards up on the right.'

Ethan stopped the car as the lights changed and Nora's mind raced to try and come up with something to break the crazy sense of anticipation creeping in.

'Eleanor really said she'd be in touch within the next couple of days?' she asked, her voice higher in pitch than she would have liked. She had a feeling her babble-rate was about to grow exponentially, and she hated the fact that a simple attraction was the explanation.

'She really did.'

'As soon as I get back to the office I'm going to call a couple of contacts. I have a few buildings in mind for headquarters and then I need to look through the information she gave you about where she wants to base her manufacturing. There are a couple of options that become available mid-March. And there's something special I want to try and get for her, right in the middle of London's fashion district. Sort of baroque-meets-boutique, but with plenty of ground-floor space. All polished floorboards, wrought-iron work everywhere and bevelled windowpanes. High-end but perfect romantic style for a flagship store. Modern office complex and concrete and glass shopping mall is not the way to go. I'm fairly sure I'm right about this.' Finally running out of steam she glanced across at him but he was concentrating on the signals ahead. The lights changed and as Ethan drove forward, Nora's hands moved against the bag sitting on her lap. 'So we're coming up to the office. There'll never be any parking around at this time of day. You can drop me off in the middle of the—hey.'

Ethan calmly drove until he reached the next junction, turned the car around and drove back so that he could ease the car to a halt right outside the back entrance to her offices. Where, for the first time in recorded history, there was an empty parking space, complete with meter. He switched off the engine and calmly turned to look at her.

'Do you know, I have a feeling you were about to nip out into the middle of the traffic and run off, and all without setting up a meeting to discuss Ryan.'

'Oh. Well.' She couldn't quite meet his eyes. How could she have forgotten who it was that had brought him to her office this morning? Was she so obsessed with KPC at the moment that nothing else could intrude? Or was it that in the space of a hundred yards, it had become awkwardly apparent to her that breathing in his scent and getting herself all stirred up was making it impossible to concentrate on anything but him. She needed to get out of this car. She needed space to be able to clear her head. Sephy was right. She really was out of practice at talking to men. 'So. Thank you for this morning. If I could grab my laptop and the information Eleanor left you with..?'

'What's the hurry?'

'No hurry. Well, I do have a lot of work to do. Why don't you phone me with a time for us to discuss Ryan. You must be really exhausted by now—'

'I'm really "something" right now. Not sure "exhausted" is the word, though.'

'Sorry. I didn't mean to come across as rude. I—' she tailed off when she saw smouldering blue eyes track their way to her lips. *I have to get out of this car before I do something properly stupid, like climb over onto your lap, grab you by the lapels of that sinfully sexy blue suit you fill out so well and give in to this insane need to touch my lips to yours.*

She was being utterly ridiculous, of course. She was supposed to be offering up a business-like thank you. Not wanting to devour a man she'd just met. Maybe if she hadn't caught sight of his chest packed with all that tight, hard muscle in her bathroom. *Yes, Nora. Absolutely blame the pecs.* But honest to God, he'd looked so good standing there, was it any wonder she'd lost her professional A game?

Biting down on her bottom lip again she tried to ignore his scent. The smile. The body. When he wasn't using all that muscle helping people he was probably working out in his own gym. Yes, that body…she mentally swooned, picked herself up and gave herself a little slap.

Never mind the package, get with the programme. None of this should be on her radar right now. Her sole focus should be on KPC. 'I don't know how to thank you for all your help.'

'You don't?'

At his quiet, teasing question, Nora dragged her gaze to his. Oh, not fair. It turned out that when Ethan Love actually wanted a person to know what he was thinking, he had no problem letting his eyes do the talking.

She simply didn't understand why he was able to affect her so, but his charm offensive was leaving her with no other option than to hastily erect her official Deflector Shield.

'Ethan, I—'

'Have to go?' he asked with an indulgent smile on his face.

'Uh-huh.' Like soonest. A few minutes more and she'd be simpering, whimpering and quite possibly whispering heated instructions as to where he could put those beautiful hands of his.

What on earth was wrong with her? She closed her eyes and pictured herself surrounded by her Deflector Shield. The one she employed when she panicked that she was getting side-tracked from her goals in life.

'Okay. You're excused,' Ethan said grinning. 'It was nice meeting you, Princess. I'll be in touch.'

Nora looked at him suspiciously. Perhaps he was bored bouncing off her official Deflector Shield because he seemed to be letting her off the hook. Which was a good thing, she reminded herself. He was Love-Rat's brother.

Way, way too complicated.

Tearing her gaze away, she refused to acknowledge the slice of bitter disappointment that she felt. She glanced up at the impressive steel and glass construction that housed KPC. That was where she belonged. Not down here in this intimate space with a man who slipped past her Deflector Shields and was connected to her family.

She let the seatbelt drag through her fingers as she released the buckle, and, muttering a heartfelt 'thank you', exited the car.

She was halfway up the shallow steps at the rear of the building when she heard his amused and oh-so-casual, 'Oh, Nora?'

She couldn't help herself. Her head whipped around at the sound of her name, which sounded like a warm invitation on his lips.

Chapter Three

Ethan was at the bottom of the stairs, holding the Moorfield bag out to her. 'This should help you out with the separation anxiety.'

Nora eyed the bag as it swung tantalisingly back and forth from his forefinger.

'Eleanor asked me to pick out something that I thought represented you best,' he told her. 'I think she was rather expecting to get a handle on you by the shoes you wore.'

Nora's eyes narrowed speculatively.

'She was a little thrown when she got me instead of you,' Ethan continued. 'But I assured her I was up to the challenge.'

Wait, he had picked out shoes for her? Was he kidding? She stared at him. He wasn't. He really wasn't. For what seemed like the hundredth time that morning she could feel herself getting all heated, flustered and distracted. That enticingly sexy shoe bag had been sitting there on the back seat of his car the entire drive back. Had he been thinking of her wearing what he'd chosen every time that slow devilish smile had come out to play? She snatched the bag and clutched it to her chest.

'Don't you want to open it up and check what I chose for you?' Ethan asked with a look that said he knew damn well she was practically salivating to open it.

'I'm super busy,' she muttered inanely, needing her will to hold out just a little longer because he looked way too sure of himself and she was feeling…so much less sure and quite possibly a little punch-drunk on him.

'Uh-huh, well I think you're going to take the lift instead of the stairs and you're going to be looking in that bag before you're in your office.'

Nora, clasped the bag tighter to her, gave him her haughtiest look and then turned on shaky legs to walk into the KPC offices.

Don't you dare look back, Leonora King. Don't you dare.

It wasn't until much later that afternoon that she realised she had left her own carrier bag, containing the remnants of her shoe, on the front seat of her car. How could she have done that? Had she subconsciously wanted to leave part of her in his car so that he would continue to think about her? Wasn't the fact that he'd picked out shoes for her enough?

She rose abruptly and went over to where she had mutinously stashed the Moorfield bag earlier. Glancing around, she decided to store it behind her door, where it couldn't continue cluttering up the place. She would *not* look inside until she'd put in a good afternoon's work. Better yet, she wouldn't look until she was back in the safety of her own apartment, where she could have whatever reaction she wanted to have in private.

Her thoughts inevitably returned to the shoe she'd left in Ethan's car and she sighed, quite disgusted with herself. She was now seriously worried that in the space of one day she had turned into some sort of sad Cinderella cliché.

The phone on her desk rang and she pounced on it, glad of the interruption. 'Yes?'

'I have Eleanor Moorfield on the line for you,' Fern said with a tiny telltale trill of excitement in her voice.

'Thanks, Fern. Pop her through.' The hand that had only that morning been attached to her shoe pressed on her stomach to try and still the rampaging butterflies. 'Eleanor? Lovely to hear from you. I was just going through the information you left with

Ethan.' At least she would have been if she hadn't been thinking about Ethan.

'Wonderful. It was a pleasure to meet Ethan.'

What did that mean? 'He did a good job, then?'

'Oh, he did a great job, really made me feel like he understood my needs,' Eleanor confirmed in a voice that almost sounded purring.

Nora bristled. She just bet he did.

'He's a great asset to have. It was astute of you to bring him on board.'

Nora's mouth felt dry. Perhaps now would be a good time to apologise for not being at the meeting in person. Explain to her that, technically, Ethan didn't work for KPC. 'I'm so pleased the meeting sounds as if it was constructive, but I feel I must apologise for not being there myself—'

'No need to worry. Ethan explained everything.'

'He did?' Nora didn't think it was possible for her heart to beat any faster. What, exactly, had Ethan said?

'Mmn—don't worry about it. I tend to go by my gut instinct and after what I saw today I'm happy to start my lawyers looking at contracts. Think you can get one to me by the end of the week?'

Nora's hand clenched against her stomach. She had thought letting Ethan help her today had been about family, but maybe *her* gut instinct had finally kicked back in. 'No problem at all. You want me to throw in a transition package for releasing the property you already own in Italy, or do you have someone handling that for you already?'

There was a smile in Eleanor's voice as she said, 'You're very good at this. Go on then, I'll take a look.'

She *was* good at this, wasn't she? Nora grinned like a Cheshire cat, feeling lighter than she had in weeks. 'I'll have one of my corporate solution professionals phone you to discuss your requirements.'

'Okay. I really want to push forward with this. I'm happy to listen as long as you don't start wanting to move my entire company into some cold City office tower. I assume you're open to discussion about the finer points?'

'Of course. Absolutely.'

'And if I want to I can deal with you directly? I may not like being handed over to a posse of staff as soon as I sign on the dotted line.'

'Well, I usually assign a personal account manager, but of course I'll make myself available if you feel something isn't being handled appropriately.'

Nora's mind whirled. Ethan hadn't simply given a good presentation; he'd saved the day and clinched the deal. It seemed an official upgrade to Mr Knight in Shining Armour was in order. She wanted to whoop for joy when she thought about being able to announce to the board who she'd snagged as their latest client. And if some of the property in Italy was worth hanging on to, their property portfolio would get a healthy bump, too. Barely managing to cling to any semblance of professionalism, she heard Eleanor speak again.

'I'm having a little party next week, a celebration for being back in London. You should come. Bring Ethan, too.'

'I'd love to. Um, I can't vouch for Ethan. He's very busy,' she excused.

'Well I'd love for him to be there, there are a lot of people I'd like to introduce you both to. It won't feel like a proper celebration without him. I'll send invitations out to you.'

Nora didn't have to work very hard to read between the lines: Ethan was expected there. 'I'll see what I can do,' she answered in her best non-committed tone. 'And thanks again, you won't regret having KPC handle all your property needs.'

Nora replaced the handset and pressed her hands to her lips. The grin started somewhere deep inside her chest and worked its way quickly up to her lips. Could it be true? Was it possible that a day that had started so abysmally could have turned around so fantastically?

She spun in her chair.

She'd done it. She'd actually done it.

Or rather, Ethan had done it.

Feeling dizzy, she stopped spinning and rose to pick up her bag as an overwhelming need to buy Ethan a special thank you present filled her.

Opening the office door she saw Fern tapping away on her keyboard. 'Why don't you switch everything off and finish early?'

Fern looked up at her with a frown. 'It's 5:55pm.'

'And that's early by your standards. Go on. Go home and phone the boyfriend. Maybe cook some pasta, open a bottle of wine…'

Fern smiled. 'Well if my boss is ordering me, who am I to disagree? I take it the phone call went well?'

'Ethan certainly seems to have charmed Eleanor Moorfield, so keep your fingers crossed.'

'That's wonderful.' She took in the handbag Nora was holding. 'Where are you off to, then?'

'Quick shopping trip and then back here for some more work.'

'Uh-huh. Okay. Or…you could go another way, and, say, stop by a certain hotel, where a certain hot guy might be staying—'

Nora's eyes narrowed a fraction.

'—to, you know,' Fern continued, cautiously, when she deciphered the warning look, 'discuss his brother.'

'Good night, Fern,' Nora said, mock sternly. 'I do not expect you to be here when I get back.'

'Yes, boss. Um, you might need your coat?'

Nora rolled her eyes, thinking that her head was all over the place. Popping back into her office, she dragged her coat off the coat-stand and was about to turn around and head straight back out the door when she spotted the Moorfield bag. An image of her standing in front of a hotel room with a bottle of champagne, wearing only her coat and whatever was in that bag sizzled and then her eyes crossed. Yes—because turning up at the door of a man you had only met that morning with nothing but a bottle of champagne, a coat and a pair of shoes, was such a subtle message, wasn't it? She could only imagine her sister's face when she had to explain quite how well Ethan and she were acquainted. Wracking her brain she tried to remember if Sephy had ever mentioned Ethan when she'd been seeing Ryan. Not that during those years Sephy and her had been sisters who'd confided everything. Mostly Nora had used university as an escape from dealing with the fallout of Jared leaving and Sephy, well, she'd kind of used Ryan as her escape. After graduating Nora had spent all her energy immersing herself in KPC, working hard to ensure no one could ever accuse her fast-track through the business as not being fully earned. Then things with Sephy and Ryan had fallen apart when she'd got pregnant with Daisy and Nora had launched straight into over-protective mode.

She wondered what Ethan and Ryan's relationship was like. It must be solid if he had flown all the way from Italy, but surely Ryan was all right if Ethan could take the time to help her out first before discussing it?

Bundling into her coat, Nora bid Fern goodnight again and made her way down the stairs and out into the cold evening air to hail a taxi. Once she was in the vicinity of the large department stores that stayed open late, she got out and wandered over to the first huge display window she came to.

Sometimes she couldn't imagine ever working anywhere but in the centre of London. Amongst the buzz and the hustle and the bustle.

Although, lately, whenever she made it back to her fabulous apartment with its views over the Thames, she felt drained from being so switched on all the time, as if she had only two modes: full-on or empty. At least full-on mode didn't give her time to think or feel. And if the emptiness started to overwhelm, she always had the family home to visit.

She stared, unseeing, at the goodies on the other side of the plate-glass window. Surely her mother had been joking about selling the forty-acre family estate in Heathstead, twenty miles outside London? Nora knew it had to be hard—understood that despite the fact that the hospital bed and nursing equipment was now gone, the memory of Jeremy King's last months were frozen very much at the forefront of her mother's thoughts. But the house stood for so much more. It had been in the family for generations. Where her father had lived for KPC, her mother had breathed life back into the estate and even now Sephy and Daisy lived in the specially built three-bedroom apartment built over the vast garages. Where would they go if her mother decided to sell? Where would her mother go? Was she really ready to leave the place she had spent years loving and tending so that it thrived as a home. What if Jared decided that one day he and Amanda wanted to come back to the UK? Surely as the eldest of the Kings, the house reverted to him? The will-reading had probably gone through this, but at the time she hadn't really paid attention. The only specifics she'd registered were that KPC wasn't affected and that Jared, Sephy and she had each received a letter from their father.

She shivered and walked to the next department store, determined to move away from thoughts that tugged at the veil of numbness she had got so good at wearing since her father's death.

Work. Work was what would see her through. Work was the only fitting way to honour her father and feel his loss less.

Sephy and Jared had already opened their letters.

She wasn't ready yet.

Not that she had to *ever* open the letter, she counseled herself as the curtain of grief threatened to descend.

All the time she kept the letter sealed, his silence wasn't final.

Nora exhaled to try and loosen the tension. Hopefully while her mother was in New York helping with Jared and Amanda's wedding plans she'd forget all about the idea of selling.

As her breath formed a foggy circle in the window of the store in front of her, she lifted her hand and, with her sleeve, brushed the condensation clear. She didn't have time to think about something that might not even happen. All she had time for lately was to deal with what was immediately in front of her while she kept all her work plates spinning in the air and right now, what was in front of her was what to send the knight-errant? Suddenly she spotted a square glass vase and, smiling, she realised she knew exactly what to fill it with. Back at the office, she unpacked the half-dozen silk ties and arranged them in the glass vase. Tying a ribbon around the vase, she added a gift tag and wrote: 'Thank you for all your help today. These are more practical than flowers and will last longer. Nora King.' She put the unusual arrangement into a presentation box and phoned a courier to have it delivered.

The next morning Nora was at her desk struggling with her concentration levels when her mobile phone rang. Answering it, she took a fortifying sip of her vanilla latte, 'Mmmn,' it was good.

'Interrupting something?' said the relaxed, earthy baritone into her ear.

Nora smiled to herself as her stomach, recognizing Ethan's voice, performed a perfect scoring six in the vault.

'Who is this?' she teased.

'You always send gifts to men you don't know?'

Ha. She wondered what he would have to say if he had even an inkling that she'd been toying with turning up at his hotel with a bottle of champagne, a pair of shoes and a very different kind of gift in mind.

'Oh.' She took another sip of coffee. 'It's you.'

'So, thanks for the "flowers".'

'You're welcome.'

Leaving her desk, she wandered over to the full-length mirror on the back of her bathroom door to check her appearance. As she saw the flush on her cheekbones she asked herself what the hell she was doing. She was preening and he couldn't even see her.

'In point of fact they're a bit of a distraction,' Ethan murmured as if a bit disconcerted her gift had such power over him.

'I'm sorry to hear that.' Although, if she was being perfectly honest, didn't she love the idea of him being as distracted by her as she was by him? Don't tell me a simple vase of ties is preventing you from having a good night's sleep?'

'Little bit, yeah. How about you? Having trouble getting your work done?'

She looked at herself in the mirror. The blush was still there, and now that she peered closer, she could tell her eyes had just a touch more sparkle. How honest should she be? It's not as if he could see she was primping, or that she needed extra coffee to get her mind off him and onto her work.

Self-preservation kicked in. 'To be honest I'm kind of swamped with the Moorfield account.'

'Yes, but are you having trouble getting any work done?'

Damn the man.

'Little bit, yeah,' she responded in kind.

'How about coming out to play, for a while?'

'Absolutely not,' she answered quickly. 'I have far too much to do.' It was for the best. She'd already issued herself with a written warning containing an embargo on Ethan Love fantasies, which were, she had told herself in her strictest most super-stern voice, all the things inappropriate.

'Shame. So what did you think of the goodie-bag contents?'

No way. Her gaze flew to her feet in the mirror. 'I haven't got around to looking yet.'

'Liar.' His soft chuckle had her flushing scarlet. His voice dropped an octave lower, 'So what did you think? Did I get you right?'

'I have to go now. I'm incredibly busy. Goodbye.' She ended the call on the sound of more deep laughter.

Had he got her right? Had he ever. If she'd had to guess, she'd have said that Ethan Love wasn't a man drawn to the obvious, so she wasn't surprised he'd avoided black. Instead he'd chosen the most sinfully gorgeous deep wine-coloured patent peep-toe stiletto sling-backs she'd ever laid eyes on. They fitted her feet as though they'd been specially made for her and in them she felt, confident, capable, utterly in control…and the tiniest bit wicked.

Wearing them so wasn't helping her not to think about him. Did he know that? He'd laughed as if he knew that.

Her phone beeped to signal an incoming text: I'm staying at The Grand. Meet me in the bar for drinks at 8pm. Wear the shoes.

Nora was tempted to tell him she'd wear whatever she damn well wanted to wear, *if* she was so inclined to meet him, that was.

Her phone beeped again and she looked down at the new text: Little Joke. The shoes are optional. But I do need to discuss Ryan with you.

Oh. Of course he did. Why did she keep forgetting that? She needed not to do that again. Ethan had something he needed to run past her about Ryan and she needed to be alert for that in order to look out for Sephy. Piqued at her ability to keep turning their interaction into something more she texted back: it'll have to be 9pm. There. That was less like "date" time and more like simply meeting-up time.

At seven minutes past nine that evening Nora walked into the hotel's bar, wearing the same designer business suit she'd put on after her gym session at 6a.m. that morning. It had been hard enough concentrating on exercising knowing Ethan owned the private leisure club in the basement of her building, but she wasn't changing for Ethan Love. This wasn't a date.

Okay, so she'd kept on the shoes he'd picked out for her, but he could read into that whatever he wanted. She knew she was wearing them because they were beautiful and comfortable. That was absolutely the only reason.

Probably.

She spotted him immediately. He was seated at the gleaming ebony bar, watching the TV screen and either oblivious to the number of women casting their eyes over him, or so used to it, he no longer noticed when he was being checked out. Her gaze flickered to the screen and she saw that he was watching a news report on the earthquake in northern Italy. She slowed her pace so that she could study him while he watched the news report. To anyone paying loose attention he seemed utterly relaxed and only vaguely interested. But, to Nora, those magnificent shoulders of his got a little tighter and sat a little higher the longer he watched.

Suddenly he turned, his gaze zeroing straight in on her and she could see nothing of the news report behind his blue eyes, only a sort of lazy warmth with a streak of sexy intensity that set off a seductive sense of anticipation in her and pulled her the rest of the way across the room to him.

He rose from his bar stool when she drew up alongside him. His head tipped in greeting and when his gaze dropped to her feet and she registered the appreciative look on his face, there was an absurd little loosening within her.

'What would you like to drink?' he asked, his eyes taking their time to travel back up to her face.

'Jack Daniel's and coke.'

He repeated her order to the bartender and swung his attention back to her. 'Tough day at the office?' he asked with empathy as he ran his gaze back over her in assessment.

'Isn't every day?' she answered with feeling and definitely without thinking. Guilt coursed through her, leaving a tremor in its wake. What was it her father used to say? If you didn't have at least one sweaty-palm feeling a week, then you weren't pushing yourself hard enough. She seemed to have upped the ratio to once a day. He'd have been proud. She frowned at the strange unfurling in her stomach because she loved the work. Of course she did.

To combat thinking about KPC and her father and centre her thoughts back on why she was here meeting with Ethan, she picked up the tumbler the bartender had set down in front of her and brought the short black straw to her lips.

She watched Ethan watching her and couldn't be certain whether it was the hit of alcohol responsible for spreading fire through her or the effect caused when his blue eyes hooded. Releasing the straw she swallowed dry air.

With a subtle clearing of her throat she fought to get a grip before she made a complete fool of herself and coughed and spluttered her way through the contents of her glass. Breaking eye contact would probably help. She brought the straw to her lips and deliberately looked around the room as she took a second careful sip.

Ethan picked up his own glass and steered them towards a small table for two in the furthest corner of the room. Once again, Nora tried to remember that this was not a date. This was a meeting to discuss his brother.

A meeting that definitely didn't warrant searching Ethan's eyes for bonus content while she returned his looks with what she was a little worried could be construed as a hint of puppy-dog adoration.

Ethan pulled out her chair and opened up with, 'So how's Sephy these days?'

'How's Ryan?' she countered, not about to give him information on her sister before she knew why he needed her help. She sat down, determined to ignore the heat of his hand as it brushed against her back.

Ethan smiled and lowered his powerful frame into the chair opposite and then took his time lifting his glass before pausing to watch her over the rim. 'Everything's fast with you isn't it?' he said, enjoying the blush that bloomed on her cheeks. 'It's a Friday night. No reason we can't unwind a little. Do the "How was your day" thing, first.'

He watched her lips purse with impatience at being made to march to another's schedule, but he liked the fact that she wasn't able to remain impassive. She'd been sneaking into his thoughts all day and he'd found himself wanting to check on her. See if he could catch the ball of pain he'd seen bouncing at the outer recesses of her eyes and throw it out of sight for her.

'Fine,' she said, shrugging her shoulders with a graceful nonchalance. 'My day was busy. How was yours?'

'Similar.' In between putting things in place for his brother, he'd spent hours on the phone trying to find out how things were in Italy. The news showed that there had been another aftershock and more buildings had collapsed. He told himself Pietro was safe and had been reunited with his family. Opting to focus on who he was with and what he needed to say, he began, 'Given your family's recent bereavement I wanted to be able to gauge how Sephy was before I gave her the news about Ryan.'

'Oh. Well. Sephy's doing fine. She handles everything life throws at her.'

'Good to know. Still,' Ethan watched Nora closely, 'grief visits people differently. I was sorry to hear about your father.'

She went utterly still, as if she hadn't expected the common courtesy from him and he told himself he didn't care what she thought about him.

'Thank you,' she eventually whispered, her smile determined as she tucked her hair behind her ear and sat up straighter. 'Let's get back to why we're here, shall we? What's going on with Ryan?'

Fixing his gaze on her, he breathed in, and said matter-of-factly, 'Ryan is in rehab.'

Nora blinked. Twice. Oh, she had impeccable manners, but between the blinks Ethan caught something else that looked a lot as though her low opinion had simply been confirmed.

'I…see,' she said quietly.

Ethan could see a question forming at the back of her mind. She was busy asking herself if this was a brother-like-brother situation; it wasn't the first time he'd been compared to Ryan – people always felt the need to lump family together – no doubt it wouldn't be the last.

Still.

Disappointment weighed heavy in his gut before he asked himself why she should be different to anyone else. 'No you don't, but that's okay,' he returned lightly. What was the point in reacting?

'Am I allowed to ask what he's in rehab for?'

He hesitated because he wasn't yet used to saying it. 'He's exhausted, very low and...has a gambling addiction.'

Again there was the blinking, before she said, 'Did you know he had a problem? I mean, did you put him in rehab or did he put himself there?'

'He mostly put himself there. I merely helped with the finer details. And, yes, I guess I suspected he had some issues, although I didn't know about the gambling. More about women and generally living beyond his means—which, let's say, weren't inconsiderable.' Especially if you counted the funds Ethan had unwittingly supplied, thinking he was simply short of cash-flow. When he thought about how he'd given Ryan money no questions asked he was disgusted with himself. Talk about carbon-copy behaviour of how his parents dealt with every problem their sons ever brought to them as children.

He lifted his glass and took a sip. At least Ryan was answering his questions and giving him the opportunity to help him now.

Nora frowned. 'Not inconsiderable,' she mumbled his words back at him. 'Is he in rehab because he reached that lowest point—has he lost everything?'

Ethan inclined his head. 'Pretty much, yeah.'

Nora whistled softly. 'That explains that, then.'

'Explains what?'

'Sephy hasn't received any child support for Daisy for months.'

Ethan took the family shame deep into his bones. It was one thing for Ryan to ruin his own life, but his daughter's? He knew Ryan had never been in Daisy's life and, given how honest his brother had been with him about how he'd been living, Ethan was actually pleased about that. But to not even pay support? 'I didn't know that. I'll take care of it immediately.'

'Don't be silly. Sephy won't accept any money from me or my brother, so I'm pretty sure she won't take any from you.'

'But the money isn't for her. It's for Daisy.'

'Do you think I haven't pointed that out to her? Neither Daisy nor Sephy go without. But Sephy is very proud. From the moment Ryan ran, she set about coping on her own. She insists she isn't bothered that Ryan hasn't paid anything towards Daisy. Of course it might be that she believes that Ryan made his choice. He was either in, or he was out, and if he was out, then it was less messy to make it all out.'

Ethan considered her words carefully. If Sephy didn't want anything to do with Ryan how was she going to react to his plan? 'Would she stop Ryan from seeing Daisy?' he asked.

'Absolutely not. Like I said, it was always more that Ryan was never particularly interested in seeing Daisy, and Sephy has always believed you can't force people to love their children,' she paused and he could see those little cogs of hers whirring and turning. 'But, surely he doesn't want Daisy to visit as part of his recovery programme? I have to tell you now that there's no way I'm going to help you persuade Sephy to allow that. Daisy is way too young to be introduced to her father for the first time in a rehab facility.'

'Relax. That's not why I wanted to see you,' he paused and then decided he might as well lay everything on the table. 'Ryan is going to need somewhere to stay when he's completed his programme.'

Nora gaped. 'You can't be serious.'

He had to hand it to her. She caught on quick.

'I'm very serious. I don't want him living back where he's been, there's too much temptation around, too many old friends willing to suck him back into that lifestyle. What I would like is to set him up with a house and a job in Heathstead. I know your sister still lives there. Ryan wants to change. He's doing all that he can do to change. I figure, give him an environment where the possibility of making a fresh start somewhere familiar is more tempting than the old life he's working so hard to distance himself from, won't hurt.'

She leant back in her chair for a second, an assessing look on her face. 'Have you actually run this past Ryan? Or is he simply another hop on the "Ethan Love Rescue Tour"?'

His fingers tightened against his glass. 'You think I like playing the hero?'

'Oh, I'm pretty sure I know you do.'

He took a couple of moments to ensure his breathing evened out. 'Whatever. This is about my brother. He asked for my help. There was no way I wasn't going to step up and do everything I could to make it possible for him to lead the life he wants to, not the one he's been addicted to. He and I have had some pretty tough conversations lately and I know he doesn't want his addiction to rule his life any longer.'

'So you want me to convince Sephy I think it's a good idea he move back near her? What if he can't maintain his programme and starts gambling again—?'

'Only he can control that. But I believe he really wants to change.' He'd never seen his brother so quietly resolved, so singularly committed and he was proud of him.

'—only this time it's worse,' Nora continued as if he hadn't spoken. 'This time his daughter gets to see him ruin his life. I'm not sure that's a risk worth taking.'

'He would have everything he needed to help him keep making the right life choices—a home, a daughter, a job, a support system.'

'A support system? Exactly how full a role are you expecting Sephy to play in this sham?'

'Again, not where I was going,' Ethan rebuked. 'Ryan has a girlfriend who would move down with him.'

'A girlfriend?'

Ethan winced. Yeah, should have waited to impart that particular snippet. Ryan's girlfriend wasn't involved in gambling and had proved herself supportive to Ryan when Ethan had checked up on her.

'Oh, this just gets better. So let me see if I have this right. You want me to help Sephy be okay with the idea that the father of her child, whom she hasn't seen for years, should get to come back to her home town to live the shiny new life his brother has arranged for him…with his girlfriend?'

He wondered if she had any idea that she sort of glowed when she was spitting mad.

He also wondered if she realised that everything she had said led him to believe Sephy would be much more open to his plan, than her. Nora was mainly coming cross like an over-protective mother bear. 'Look, I get that you want to protect your sister but you won't make me believe there's anything between Sephy and Ryan now. Sephy is in a position, however, to make it simple for Ryan to go about leading the best life he can. For their daughter.'

Nora's eyes thundered. '*This* is why you really helped me yesterday. So you could gain leverage. You scratched my back so I should scratch yours?'

Ethan hardly ever responded to anger but he was damned if he was going to sit here and let her get away with casting him as some sort of villain. 'Is that really why you think I helped you?' he asked slowly.

He watched the way she had her hands on the table, curled around her glass like a lifeline, and his own hands, as if drawn by magnet, moved to within touching distance of hers.

'You sure you're determined to ignore what's also going on here?' he asked, making his voice quiet. Intimate.

Her eyes flicked to his and then flicked sharply away again. 'I don't know what you mean.'

'Oh, you definitely do, but let's see what happens if I decide to call your bluff.' Slowly, his little finger stroked deliberately against the side of her hand.

Her white-knuckled grip on the glass slackened a little and for a heartbeat he really thought she was going to reciprocate. Really *wanted* her to reciprocate. But in the next instant she was removing her hands from the table altogether and placing them on her lap.

'I'm sorry. It's commendable that you're looking out for your brother this way, but I have to do what's best for my sister and niece and I can't agree with what you want to do for Ryan. Maybe when he's finished rehab and can demonstrate he's readjusted. I hope he fights his demons and is successful. But if you put this idea to Sephy she's going to come to me for advice. And I'm telling you right now, she listens to me.'

'We'll see.' He leant back in his chair. Assessed the flush on her skin and the shine in her eyes. 'Another drink?'

'I can't. I need to get back.' She bent down to pick up her bag and then pushed back her chair. There was a stubborn tilt to her chin that he found fascinating.

'Pressing date?' He asked rising from his chair.

'Work.'

His grin was quick to form. 'Before you go,' he said, grasping her arm loosely, halting her movement in its tracks as she went to walk by. 'I helped you for two reasons, starting with because I could and ending with because I'm attracted to you.'

Chapter Four

'Where are you?' Nora muttered under her breath as she pressed Sephy's doorbell for the second time and then stepped back to glance over the railing to where her sister's little runabout was parked. The car was here so she must be in. Maybe she was up at the main house.

After leaving her second voicemail message that morning, Nora had given up trying to get her sister on the phone and had decided to drive down instead and tell her about Ryan face to face.

She went to press the doorbell again.

'Hello?' said her niece from behind the door.

Finally. Nora practically flung herself at the front door. 'Daisy? Sweet Pea, its Auntie Nora. Can you go and get Mummy to open the door, please?'

There was a rustling sound at her feet and Nora looked down to find a twelve-inch princess doll being posted through the cat flap at the base of the door.

Oh no. She really didn't have time to play princess-escapes-drudgery-of-castle-life-through-drawbridge-and-sets-off-on-grand-adventure. Picking up Princess Belle she looked down at her enviously, 'It's all right for you in your shiny yellow gown,' she accused. 'You get to spend your day without a care in the world. You don't have to tell your sister her issue-ridden ex, who

48

abandoned her and her daughter, is about to move back to town with his girlfriend. Yes. With his girlfriend. What do you think she's going to say about that? What?' She brought Princess Belle to her ear. 'No words of wisdom? Is that because Sephy could go either way—or,' Nora lowered the princess doll from her ear and scowled down at her, 'perhaps because I am talking to an inanimate object.'

Bending down again, she attempted to post the doll back through the cat-flap. Clearing her throat, she adopted her best royal-princess voice and said, 'Brr. It's too chilly to be outside today. I must return to the warmth of my castle where a responsible adult can make me a lovely hot strong cup of coffee.'

The door swung open and Nora had a glimpse of Daisy hopping up and down with excitement before the little girl disappeared out of sight.

'It looks like the princess is in need of a knight in shining armour to assist.'

Nora's head whipped up at the sound of Ethan's voice.

'Your princess-to-princess plea was very entertaining,' he added when her mouth dropped open but no words came out.

As she rose from her crouching position she couldn't help cataloguing muscular legs with a dusting of hair, obscured from the mid-thigh up by a soft and inviting black robe. A black robe, which, if she wasn't very much mistaken, she had given to her sister at Christmas. Why the hell wasn't he wearing any proper clothes? Did he even have on anything under the robe? And what the hell was he even doing here? Oh my God! Please don't say Sephy had let him move in while he tried to convince her to help his brother? She knew her sister was generous but that was too much. How the hell had he got here so quickly, anyway? And why did he look so at home? And again…no clothes…what the hell?

'Left your superhero costume back at the hotel?' she clipped out, unable to help herself. But really, she reasoned, she'd spent the entire drive down torturing herself with supposedly calming classical music in the vain hope that it would get her mind off the man and now he was here and already in rescue mode?

Ethan answered with a grin. He leant his arm against the door-frame as if he owned the place and when her gaze was helplessly drawn to the way the robe parted across his spectacularly broad chest she was reminded of how she'd felt when he'd told her last night that he was attracted to her. Of how his blatancy had tempted her, so that for a moment she'd felt completely free of the grief she carried around, free of all the worry about the business. Free of everything except the desire to respond to him and start filling up some of the holes inside her with something less…permanent.

The need had frightened her. She was fairly sure she shouldn't be thinking of Ethan as a treat to award herself because life had been tough lately.

'The elegant biker-chick looks good on you,' Ethan said, his hand gesturing loosely to her.

Running her hands down her skinny-jean-clad legs, Nora looked at the pale blue cashmere jumper she'd teamed with the black leather biker jacket and tried to think of something to say. This was like last night all over again. Ethan said something contentious and she clammed up like a novice and then wanted to run.

Last night she *had* actually run, all the way back to her apartment to keep busy and stop herself thinking about the attraction between them. She didn't understand it. Wasn't sure they even liked each other as people. All the Pilates poses she'd stretched herself into and all the looking at work reports she'd done hadn't made her feel any less cowardly for running…or any less cross with herself for being so easily tempted by someone who seemed to think everyone needed helping or rescuing. Well she could rescue herself, thank you very much. *If* she needed to. Which she absolutely did not. There was nothing wrong with her that work wouldn't put right and now that she had the Moorfield account, all she needed was to be left alone so that she could concentrate on KPC. She didn't need Ethan to pull her focus.

'Of course this isn't the first time I've seen you out of your little business suits,' Ethan added conversationally, from his entry-barring position in the doorway.

'In your imagination, maybe,' Nora snorted.

'Actually I was just looking at the photo of you and Sephy on her pin board in the kitchen.'

Nora's teeth ground together. She had a feeling she knew which photo he was referring to. Great. He got to languish around in a black silk robe that somehow emphasised his masculinity to magnificent proportion, all the while ogling a photo of her dressed as a Christmas Pudding from one of KPC's winter parties.

She really hated that photo.

'Coming in to plead your case then, Princess?' Ethan asked, holding the door open.

And she really hated him calling her "Princess". As if she hadn't had to work her arse off to get where she was. Biting her tongue, she forwent a bitchy retort in favour of warmth, which hit her immediately upon following him inside. She couldn't believe it was her following him through her sister's house and not the other way around, but as she hovered just inside the kitchen and endeavoured to thaw out, she watched and frowned as Daisy reappeared from playing in the lounge and wrapped herself around Ethan's knees. Even if Ethan had got straight into his car after meeting with her last night and driven here to speak to her sister, it was obvious that her niece felt comfortable around him. She wished she could feel so comfortable.

Nora's judgement of everyone and everything had stalled straight after the thing with her now ex-boyfriend, Steve. The thing where she'd discovered that far from the two of them being on the same page of the same book, as she'd thought, Steve had decided that the plot wasn't for him, skipped the middle and had gone straight to the end.

It was all for the best, Nora thought, repeating in her head the words she had used over and over to console herself afterwards. She looked briefly at Daisy. She wasn't losing out—she was fulfilling her ambition. She had KPC, which was all that she had wanted for the longest time.

Stopping in front of Sephy's pin board she spied the dreadful fancy-dress photo and surreptitiously slid it out to shove it, out of sight, under the printed email containing the date of Daisy's nursery-school wellie-wanging competition.

'Sephy's upstairs, but I expect she allows you to actually sit down when you visit,' Ethan said, obviously completely at ease, and Nora wondered if being comfortable in any environment was something they taught you at Disaster Response Team academy, or wherever it was he got his training to cope with whatever situation he found himself in.

Perhaps she would benefit from attending a course, because looking around the homely, cluttered kitchen, she didn't feel at home. Instead she felt more like a stranger rather than the family she was. Time to claw back some sense of familiarity. 'Daisy, where's Mummy?'

'Mummy's in bed with 'foo and we're not to wake her less it's a 'mergency,' Daisy declared importantly.

This was a 'mergency. And what the hell was 'foo anyway? Was that Daisy-speak for flu? Nora looked at Ethan. 'She went to bed and left you in charge?'

'It was more like I told her she could take a lie down for half an hour and I'd watch Daisy.' He reached to get mugs down from the shabby-chic dresser she and Sephy had bought at auction and taken hours to manoeuvre into the house. Ethan could probably have carried the entire thing up the stairs on his own and at a jog. 'You like it strong and hot, right?' he said.

Nora got caught up in the play of muscles shifting and settling under the robe he wore. *How could a woman not?* It may have been a while, but she was fairly sure she wasn't misremembering that.

Silence.

Coffee, Nora realised. The man was talking about coffee. She met his amused and knowing stare and with her tongue well and truly stuck to the roof of her mouth she could only nod.

There was a tug on her sleeve, and, mighty glad of the distraction from wondering exactly why Ethan Love was parading around her sister's home in her sister's robe, Nora looked down at Daisy.

'Auntie Nora, have you come to play?'

'Yes, Nora. Have you come to play?' Ethan coaxed.

Her gaze swung straight back to Ethan's to take in that mouth of his and the way it morphed into full-blown wickedness. She was mortified that from some simple teasing from him her body could respond with such melting interest. 'Maybe later,' she said to Daisy and fought to pull herself together. 'So what did Sephy say when you told her?' she asked of Ethan. If she focused on her sister, then surely she could steer clear of lust-land. 'You *have* told her?'

'Told me what?' came the sand-papery question from the kitchen doorway.

Nora took one look at her sister and knew she hadn't a clue as to why Ethan was here. She didn't look to be in any fit state to be told either, if the red nose, puffy eyes and the pj's she only wore when she was ill, were anything to go by. She turned to face Ethan. 'You've been here long enough to take your clothes off, but you haven't told her yet?' she whispered furiously. 'And while we're at it, just exactly why are you wearing my sister's robe?'

'Told me what?' Sephy repeated, looking from Nora to Ethan. When the two of them remained silent, Sephy sighed, pointed to her daughter and then pointed upstairs. Three sets of eyes watched as Daisy dragged Princess Belle off by the hair for another adventure.

With little ears out of range, Sephy looked at Nora and said, 'Ethan is wearing my robe because as he was getting out of the car this morning, Daisy decided to christen his visit and his clothes by landing a practice wellie-wanging throw right to his solar plexus. There was lots of mud but thankfully no blood. His clothes are in the dryer and I offered him the first thing I had to hand to help him keep warm.' One perfectly arched eyebrow rose in warning.

'Is there anything else you want to know before you tell me what's going on?'

Despite the croak in her sister's voice, Nora couldn't miss the underlying frost, or that it was aimed directly at her. The reason for the cold shoulder wasn't entirely unexpected. Being on the receiving end of a lecture from her sister the other night hadn't completely rendered her mute. She may have retaliated with a few choice remarks about Sephy's friend, Luke, and how he always seemed to be around, lately.

Nora knew her sister hated any implication she depended on anyone for help as much she herself hated any implication she might use work as an excuse not to deal with other things.

Automatically feeling bad, she responded with, 'Sorry. It's none of my business who you have to visit, or what they wear while they're here.' She turned to Ethan and with false concern added, 'I do hope you weren't hurt? So very lucky that the wellington didn't land…lower.'

'I'll survive. And, it was refreshing to discover that at least one of the King females seems to be able to part with their shoes.'

Nora went red at his reference to shoe-gate.

'What's this about shoes?' Sephy asked, 'And what's with the repartee? You two know each other?' she added, looking suspiciously from one to the other.

'No,' Nora said.

'Yes,' Ethan said at the same time.

Nora counted to ten. 'Not really. That is, Ethan stopped by KPC a couple of days ago to run something past me before—'

Understanding registered across Sephy's face. 'Before he decided to come to me. Great. What am I, like, twelve?' She turned to Ethan. 'So I take it this isn't about you being in the area and wanting to get to know my daughter.'

Ethan did at least have the grace to look chastened while Sephy wandered over to the kitchen table, pulled out a chair and sat down heavily. 'This must be about Ryan, then? What's he done?'

Ethan shot Nora a quick look she couldn't interpret as he sat down opposite her sister.

He looked as though he was analysing not only what to say but how to say it and suddenly Nora understood his reticence. Once you started unloading, that's when the questions came. Questions you didn't necessarily have the answers for. No matter how much you felt it was your responsibility to provide them.

She knew because when her brother, Jared, had left home on her nineteenth birthday all she'd had were questions. Questions her father refused to answer with anything other than the stock phrase: Jared is well but he has decided not to be part of this family any more.

In public her father had point blank refused to speak on the subject. Nora hadn't had that luxury. Every one of the simple "oh, he's on holiday" or "oh, he's off travelling for a while" had got harder and harder to say as the polite enquirers had changed into needy, greedy gossipers. With her father refusing to discuss Jared and with every attempt to push the issue only making her mother more upset, talking about Jared's absence within the family had become impossible.

Finally, when it had become apparent to her, that as a family they were never going to be able to talk about Jared reasonably, Nora had switched instead to trying to fill the gap her big brother had left behind. Filling that gap meant not drawing attention to it in the first place and she would always worry that in reinforcing her own relationship with her father, she had not only prolonged not talking about Jared but had made it into a bigger problem than it needed to be.

Part of flying out to New York to ask her big brother for help with KPC had been about trying to make up for feeling so guilty that she had been given the company when everyone knew it should have been his. It had been the hardest thing she'd ever done—to admit KPC was in trouble—to tell the brother she hadn't seen in ten years that their father was dying.

But ultimately, when she had forced the words out, Jared had done what Ethan was doing now. Regardless of what had gone on in the family, Jared had decided to help. Whatever the past. Whatever the problem. Whatever the cost. It was what a responsible person did.

As Ethan started talking, Nora finished off making the hot drinks, grabbing an extra mug for Sephy. His voice was deep and gentle but unfaltering and as she joined them at the table, pushing a mug of coffee towards each of them, Nora stole a glance at Sephy.

Her complexion was beginning to match the green walls of her kitchen and instantly she wanted to step in. 'Sephy, if you're not well enough to hear this, Ethan can come back another time.'

'No. I want to hear it all now.' She looked at Ethan. 'Carry on, Ethan.'

Nora sat down at the table and watched Sephy's face as Ethan recounted how Ryan had been living since he'd left Heathstead four years ago. Sephy had such a huge heart and since Daisy's birth it had only got larger. As Nora watched the sympathy appear she felt guilty that she was more inclined to reserve judgement.

'Don't get me wrong,' Sephy said when Ethan had finished updating her. 'I'm very glad he got help, impressed even that he started sorting help out for himself. It's a lot to take in after so much time.' She took a gulp of coffee. 'But of course I'll help in any way I can. Nora too, won't you?'

Nora frowned. 'It's not that simple,' she said quietly, knowing her sister hated her acting like the responsible sibling. But somebody had to remind Sephy that this time around, where Ryan was concerned, Sephy had a choice. She didn't have to automatically comply. She needed to think about the bigger picture. Helping out of some sense of misguided responsibility would only leave her vulnerable to being hurt if Ryan couldn't change. Nora didn't want that for her sister. What she wanted was for her sister to catch a break. Sephy liked to give the impression she could handle anything, but Nora knew she was still hurting over what their father had written to her in his letter. She didn't want to see her sister hurting over something else she couldn't control.

But how not to look like the big bossy sister, wading in?

'Of course it's that simple,' Sephy insisted. 'Or are you telling me you're too busy?'

Maybe if she did, it would at least slow things down a little. 'I do have a major client at work and—'

'Oh my God,' Sephy said, 'really? Someone in the family is in trouble and you're playing the work card?'

Nora sprang up from the table. She was mighty tempted to point out that Ryan had clearly never wanted to be a part of the King family in the first place, otherwise he wouldn't have run the minute Sephy told him she was pregnant. Why should Ethan get to come here and create that place for him? Surely Sephy was going to make Ryan earn it.

But suddenly Sephy was looking at Ethan and then looking back at her with a fascinated expression and Nora could see her sister adding two and two together and coming up with twenty. Her heartbeat escalated alarmingly.

No. See. Her reluctance to throw her name into the helping hat was in no way connected to the man sitting across from them at the table.

How could Ethan possibly be a factor in what was, to her, a perfectly logical wish to protect her sister from rushing in and getting hurt?

She tried communicating that via a combination of subtle staring and full-on glaring. When that didn't work she scooted over to the kitchen doorway and jerked her thumb to show she expected her sister to follow her out. There was no way she was going to go hammer and tongs at her sister in front of Ethan. When Sephy didn't immediately get up from the table and follow her, Nora glowered and gesticulated harder.

Sephy sighed, and with an apologetic look at Ethan that made Nora want to scream, picked up her mug and got up from the table to follow her into the hall.

As soon as they were both out of Ethan's earshot the words Nora had wanted to say fell from her lips in a barely controlled whisper, 'That's it? Of course you'll help? It's that easy for you? *Love-rat* left, but he gets to come back? Just like that?' Nora couldn't believe that at the behest of his brother, Ryan was so easily getting a second chance. Or that Sephy wasn't worried about what might happen if she gave him a second chance.

'He's not coming back to *me*, you idiot. Didn't you hear Ethan say he has a girlfriend? Oh,' Sephy put a hand out and clutched Nora's forearm as the anger visibly drained out of her, 'don't tell me all this time you've worried? Norsies, you know I got over Love-Rat a long time ago.'

'Of course you're over him,' Nora agreed. 'You'd be mad not to be over him after the way he treated you.'

'And let's face it, it's not as if we were ever like you and Steve, anyway.'

Nora searched deep inside for the safety blanket she called 'Numb' but it must have been in the wash, or something. Emotion started bubbling its way up to the surface. 'Steve and I were never like that, either,' Nora insisted, tamping the hurt back down with all her might. 'I don't know why everybody thought we were.'

'Right. I don't know how any of us could have got that impression. I mean, it's not as if you asked him to marry you, or anything?'

Nora stared at her sister as the emotion fizzed away in her gullet, making simple words impossible to form.

'God. Nora. I'm sorry. I shouldn't have said that as if it was a joke—'

'Forget it,' she finally got out. This wasn't about her. This was about Sephy.

'He wasn't right for you anyway,' Sephy soothed. 'Bet he didn't even score on your list.'

'List? What list?' *Oh my God. Her Love List.* That was the second time this week she'd been forced to think about something she'd written years ago, for heaven's sake. 'You're referencing something I wrote a gazillion years ago?' she spluttered. 'You see? How can I not worry when you're clearly stuck in the past?'

Sephy simply smiled gently as if Nora's clever insult harking back to the past implied she protested too much.

'We are not talking about that list—like, *ever*,' Nora hissed out. 'This is about you and the big picture. What if—'

'No "what if's". Sometimes you overcomplicate everything. He's Daisy's father, Nora.'

'I know. And you have Luke now, but—'

Sephy's eyes got all bug-shaped round. 'I don't *have* Luke. Luke is not for having—there is no Luke and I—I really need you to shut up about this stupid Luke stuff.'

'Okay. Okay,' Nora pacified, feeling bad when Sephy broke into a coughing fit. 'You don't talk about Steve. I won't talk about Luke. Let's get back to Ryan. Why do you want to help him?'

Sephy thought for a while and then, her voice a low whisper, said, 'Because if Ryan ever wants to re-engage with Daisy, then I want that too. I don't want her feeling as if her father has no time for her. That his other interests take priority or as though she has to shine brighter for his attention.'

Lord. Nora reached out to squeeze her sister's arms. 'You do know Dad loved you to pieces, right?'

Sephy's smile turned watery. 'Well, he loved me for sorting my life out and he loved Daisy, at any rate.'

'Sephy, he loved you for you. What he wrote you—' Nora held her hands up helplessly.

'Was because he loved me. I know. You're right. I'm meepy with the flu, that's all.'

'And this thing with Ryan has come out of the blue,' Nora added with understanding. 'There is nothing wrong with taking some time to think this all over before you decide for certain.'

'You know I'm not like you. I don't weigh the odds. I'm entering a business deal. And I won't go to worst-case scenario and then work back from there until I end up not taking the risk in the first place.'

Nora stared at her sister. Was this what Sephy thought she did now—went to worst-case scenario straight from the off? When had she started playing it so safe? *Why* had she started playing it so safe? But deep down she knew. It had started when Steve had turned her down, telling her she was already married. To her job. Then the company she loved had floundered under her steerage. And playing it safe had solidified into a way of life when her father—her mentor—had died, ripping her foundation out from under her and leaving her with responsibilities she suddenly felt thoroughly ill-equipped to deal with.

Shaking her head to clear it, she said to Sephy, 'Maybe this time you should go to worst-case scenario and see if you can live with that, before you act.'

'No, I'm going with my gut. This is for Daisy as much as it is for Ryan. Besides, I'm pretty sure all Ethan is looking for from me is my blessing. I can control when and if Ryan sees Daisy.'

'Okay. But baby steps, right? If at any time you feel you've got in over your head, you'll call me?'

'You sound like Jared.'

Yes. Well. Was she supposed to gracefully slot back into being the middle child? She'd taken on the role of big sister when their big brother had left. It was a difficult role to give up. She was reminded, once again, about Ethan and what he was doing for Ryan. He was doing what every older sibling did. The responsible thing.

'Did you know Ethan when you and Ryan were seeing each other?' she asked Sephy.

Sephy shook her head and tiptoed to the kitchen doorway, poking her head around the door to look in at Ethan before looking back at Nora and whispering, 'Ryan always told me that Ethan was the good child. That he was impossible to live up to.' She stuck her head around to steal another glimpse. 'But seriously,' she said, wrenching Nora towards her so that the next thing Nora knew she was having her head shoved around the doorframe before being yanked back into the hallway. 'No one who looks that good can be that good. Know what I'm saying?'

'No, I don't know what you're saying,' Nora lied.

'I'm saying I saw the way you looked at him. I'm saying maybe you could find out if he's good or bad…and if he's bad, how good he is at being bad?'

Sephy wiggled her eyebrows suggestively and Nora snorted.

And then they both froze as they heard movement from the kitchen.

When Ethan didn't make an appearance, Nora grabbed Sephy by the arm and dragged her down the hall and further out of Ethan's earshot. 'You're insane,' she whispered frantically. 'He's Ryan's brother, which is, like, incredibly wrong. What if—'

'Oh my God, Nora,' Sephy looked utterly exasperated with her. 'The sky has been falling in since before Dad died and you've coped. You're always lecturing me on thinking before I act, well what if this one time you acted instead of thinking? What if you let yourself have some fun? It might heal you quicker than all that work you insist on burying yourself under.'

'I'm fine,' Nora insisted with a heartfelt sigh. She'd already decided that fun-shaped Ethan was not what she needed. 'You know we wouldn't keep fighting if you didn't keep thinking I had a choice about the amount of work I have to do. You seem to think running KPC is a walk in the park.'

'You're probably right,' Sephy said.

Usually the peacekeeper, Nora always tended to back down first, so when Sephy suddenly smiled and grabbed her by the shoulders to frog-march her back to the kitchen, she had a right to be suspicious. 'But with any luck,' Sephy added, 'being so uber-busy might act like a challenge to someone like Ethan. Shall we see?'

'Seraphina King, whatever screwy thing you're thinking—don't.'

Too late.

Nora felt a shove and then she was stumbling over the kitchen

61

threshold.

'Sorry,' Sephy apologised as she smiled at Ethan and sat back down at the table. 'Sisters and their little chats, you know how it is.'

'I'm not sure I do,' Ethan responded, looking slightly bemused.

Nora finally got her feet to move and joined them at the table. 'What did you have in mind for a job for your brother?'

Ethan stared at her for a few moments before obviously deciding to let her get back to the reason for his visit. 'I have a few ideas,' he said.

'Maybe Ryan could help you out with Love Leisure?' Nora suggested, thinking Ethan could keep a close eye on him that way. Ethan did, at least, seem different to what she knew of his brother. He hadn't given her the impression he ran from anything, so she was pretty sure he'd remain invested in keeping an eye on Ryan.

'It's funny you should say that.'

'You're Love Leisure?' Sephy asked with delight. 'I think I remember Ryan saying you were working abroad when we were together.'

'I probably was on and off. When I wasn't I was busy networking and securing investment for this small gymnasium near to the university I went to in Hull. The first Love Leisure. A lot of hard work later and Love Leisure has steadily grown into the type of exclusive brand that you've obviously heard of. I'm always looking for new places we could open up.'

'Ooh, we could do with a Love Leisure here in Heathstead,' Sephy said.

'Again, it's funny you should say that.'

'You're going to open up a Love Leisure facility in Heathstead? That would be perfect for Ryan. Well, Nora can definitely help you out on the property front.'

'KPC is not an estate agency,' Nora responded, wishing she could shove a 'subtle' pill down her sister's throat. She wracked her mind to come up with some sort of suitable excuse that would get her out of this twilight zone and back to somewhere where she felt more comfortable. Like the office.

'Of course it isn't,' Sephy placated. 'But you have expert knowledge of commercial property, what's a good fit and what's not. You can help Ethan source new premises.'

There was every chance that as soon as Sephy recovered from the flu, Nora was going to poke her eyes out. What part of 'whatever you're thinking—don't' hadn't Sephy heard? She was absolutely, positively, too busy to help Ethan. She didn't have time to be around him. To be pulled in by the attraction. To be 'in with fun and out with consequences'. She had work to do.

She started to feel panicky that when push came to shove she wouldn't be able to keep to the priorities she'd set herself. In possibly the worst case of acting ever, she pulled out her phone and pretended a text had come in. Staring at the screen she said, 'Excuse me. I need to phone this person back about work.'

Chapter Five

Nora unlocked one of the garage doors under Sephy's apartment and switched on the bank of overhead lights. As they flicked on one by one she walked past several classic cars until she reached the last plot, where she swept the dust cover off her beloved Bonneville T100 Triumph motorbike. Okay, so the bike really belonged to her brother. She had been sort of safeguarding it for the last decade.

Checking the bike over would hopefully sort out her dodgy equilibrium, restoring her to a King who could handle whatever was thrown at her. She ran a finger idly over the leather seat. Sometimes she thought that the tighter she held on the less in control she felt, but she had too much to lose to try any other way.

She hadn't been out on the bike since the night she'd decided to sneak out of the King winter party the December before last to get home to Steve.

She'd been living with him while Jared and Amanda stayed in her apartment in the City. True, when he'd suggested moving in together the first time, she'd put him off with an excuse about needing to find her feet at KPC. She hadn't understood the hurry. Their relationship was in a great place. They both respected the importance of working hard at their careers and the hastily arranged and hurried meetings for sex was fun. A bonus. Back then she hadn't thought long-term. She'd been happy enjoying what they had.

Staying with him while her apartment was temporarily occupied by Jared and Amanda had been convenient. Not a prelude to more. But with everything going on with KPC and the difficult time getting to know Jared again, having someone to come home to and talk with had actually been lovely and made life easier. Suddenly she'd been open to diving into a more permanent relationship with Steve.

Yeah.

Totally hadn't worked out.

Nora thought back to the Kings' winter party, remembering how the tension between Jared and her father had wound tighter and tighter. She'd been a bag of nerves. Hadn't wanted to be present if they combusted because she'd risked so much, personally, to get Jared back in the first place.

Escaping on the bike had been the outlet she'd needed.

Finding Amanda, obviously upset, on the gravel path that led away from the main house had her offering her a lift out of there and the two of them had sped away with the skirts of their ball gowns billowing behind them.

Not going out on the motorbike hadn't been a conscious decision after the death of her father.

She didn't have the time.

Nora swallowed the lie back down and walked over to a wall of racking where her helmet was stored, but the untruth pressed back at her.

Okay. That wasn't the reason she hadn't been out on the bike.

She'd been afraid that the grief she was holding inside would spill out while she was on the bike and have her either losing control or riding forever as she tried to outdistance herself from the pain of losing her father. After a while, when she'd got the grief to settle in one area deep inside, she then hadn't wanted to get on the bike for fear of inviting that sense of freedom and escape. What if she liked it too much? What if she started to need that feeling to get through the day? What if she started wanting to be on the bike more than she wanted to be at KPC each day? What if, what if, what if?

When she felt more like her old self, when the constant second-guessing had passed and things at KPC were flowing more easily she would get back on the bike.

She glanced at the gleaming chrome on the handlebars and felt the lure of the road. Maybe she was ready now. Maybe it wouldn't do any harm to pop out for a sneaky quick ride. Feel the throb of the engine. Feel the air sail past.

Introduce her new self to her old self and see if they could blend a little.

Slipping her arm through the open visor on the helmet she collected it up and then kicked the motorbike stand into the up position so that she could wheel the bike out across the garage's pristine concrete sealed floor.

When the shadow fell across her path, she looked up to see Ethan standing before her in jeans, navy cable sweater and his duffle coat. Absurdly she wondered if Sephy had watched him change after handing him his clothes from the dryer.

'This beauty belong to you?' Ethan asked, running his gaze over the machine in appreciation.

Wrenching her gaze back to the bike she said, 'I guess technically it belongs to my brother. When he went to New York I kind of took it upon myself to look after it for him.'

The summer before Jared had left he'd spent hours riding around on it and when she'd spied it in the garage she'd thought that maybe if she did the same she'd get some answers as to why he'd really left. After the first few rides she'd been smitten. Taking care of the bike had helped her feel closer to Jared.

'If you've been looking after this bike for that long then I think you can call dibs on it,' Ethan said softly.

'I guess.' She reached out and laid her hand on the bike. 'It certainly seems to respond to my handling.'

66

Ethan ran a hand over the back of his head. 'Thinking about you handling all this machine is pretty damn sexy.'

Nora had no choice but to lick her lips at his admission. 'Ethan,' she warned. Her voice low and, she hoped, definite.

'Leonora,' he countered, his sensual lips tilting upwards playfully.

Okay, how did she concentrate after that, because hearing her full name on his lips that way was, to coin a phrase, also pretty damn sexy.

'Don't.' The word left her lips in a plea.

'Why did you leave like that?' he asked.

'I had to take a work call—'

'Pretty sure you didn't,' he said and waited for her to speak as if he had all the time in the world.

Honestly. Any normal person would let her off the hook. 'If Sephy sent you out here to make sure I'm all right, you can tell her I'm fine. I'm a big girl. If something doesn't go my way I move on.'

'Yeah? If something doesn't go my way I tend to try and make it so that it does.'

That was what she was afraid of. She raised her gaze to his and determined to make this all about something other than what they might want from each other. 'Well, congratulations. You didn't have to even try to get Sephy on board. You can rest happy now that you have her blessing to move Ryan back here.'

His eyes narrowed a fraction. 'I do get it, you know. I know you're only trying to protect your sister.'

Nora sighed. 'I'm not sure why I bother, really. Sephy has always been fiercely independent.'

'Maybe she feels between you and your brother she has a lot to live up to.'

'Well that's completely ridiculous. Sephy and I aren't competitive with each other. Sephy isn't interested in the business. She has her own things.'

'Was she ever even given the chance?'

Nora thought hard. It wasn't true, was it? God. She already

felt guilty enough that when Jared had left, she'd seized upon the opportunity to finally let her father see how good she could be for the company.

'I can see that you worry about Sephy but you don't have to worry about her and Ryan,' Ethan said confidently. 'I'm not going to let Ryan hurt her, or Daisy, in any way.'

The crazy thing was that hardly even knowing him—she believed him. So she should be feeling relieved, right? Now that she was absolved from fretting over Sephy and was free to direct all her energy back into her work.

Except.

How could she possibly concentrate on her work with him being here, taking responsibility and helping where she should be helping? That was if she even got past thinking about him in the first place.

'What is it you want, Ethan?'

She wished she could identify even one of the emotions that flickered across his face before he schooled his features and employed that charming smile of his. 'I think I want you to take me out on this bike.'

'So not going to happen.'

'No? You're not interested in a ride?'

Down girl. 'Not with you. No.'

Ethan folded his arms casually in front of him. 'See now you've gone and hurt my feelings.'

'I doubt it. In any case, you're too,' Nora paused and ran her eyes over the bike and then over him, 'large.'

He threw his head back and laughed and when his gaze rested upon hers again his eyes held a potent mix of humour and heat. 'What if I promised to scoot in real tight behind you?'

Nora looked down at the bike between them. Tempted. So tempted she thought she could already imagine the delicious imprint of his body from the backs of her thighs all the way up her back.

'What if you went back on upstairs and start filling Sephy in on your grand plans instead.'

'Come on,' he cajoled, 'one ride. Sephy needs time for the news to really sink in.'

She'd told him Sephy listened to her. Yeah, she sure told him, hadn't she? There was no point letting him know Sephy had heard her trepidation but discounted it.

'What exactly is it that you have against me?' Ethan grinned. 'Or is it that you're afraid of what's happening here?'

She forced herself to meet his gaze. 'You misunderstand. I'm not afraid of anything. And why would I have anything against you?' Again, something flashed in his eyes. He really was very good at hiding his thoughts. She guessed he'd seen so much in his job that he'd got used to hiding his reactions. 'Sephy said all that stuff about me helping you because she thinks she's helping me.' *To find the 'fun' I don't have time for and don't need anyway.*

'You sure you're not afraid? Because from where I'm standing that is exactly how you look.'

'Most probably it's the lighting in here.'

He laughed again, and, heaven help her, she softened. Well, caved might be a more accurate word, because the next thing she knew she was saying, 'Oh, go over to the rack over there and grab the spare helmet.'

To avoid looking at him she concentrated on swinging her leg over the back of the bike and then buckling her helmet.

Moments later Ethan got on behind her.

His hands felt huge and warm as they settled on her waist. His hips and thighs cradled hers, making her feel delicate and fragile and causing her to drag a breath deep into her lungs. She must be mad to have even considered this. But then she was starting the ignition and gunning the engine.

By the time they'd whizzed past a few miles of scenery Nora was wondering why she'd left it so long.

The giant knot that had been lodged somewhere between her

69

stomach and throat for the past few months shifted slightly. The movement frightened her a little. She had no idea what she'd do if the knot started to uncoil. She liked her state of suspended animation. Liked how she was able to function when she was in it.

To distract from worrying about that humongous knot unravelling inside of her she rode a little harder. A little faster.

And loved it.

When she realised her face was aching because she'd actually been grinning with the rush of it all, she eased off the throttle and swung the bike into a makeshift lay-by.

Ethan's hands squeezed against her waist briefly before releasing her. She felt him remove his helmet and shift slightly to rest it on his knee. Unbuckling her own helmet she pulled it off and shook her hair out. Then, reaching up with her hand she fluffed her fingers through her layers a couple of times, telling herself the action wasn't for Ethan but simply because she didn't want tangles.

She stared out at the rolling fields in the distance and a heartfelt sigh left her body unexpectedly and without her permission.

'Yeah, that'll do it,' Ethan said as he too stared out at the view. He turned back towards her. 'Feels good. Thank you.'

Nora nodded.

'Is this land in front of us still part of the King estate?' he asked.

'No, ours lies more to the west. It's just as pretty, though,' she automatically defended.

'I'm sure it is,' Ethan replied, looking at her rather than the view he'd been asking about.

Nora tried to ignore the lick of pleasure his words provoked. Turning resolutely back to stare in front of her she wondered if her mother had mentioned selling to Sephy. Her sister certainly hadn't said anything to her about it. Nora bit her lip. She shouldn't mention it if their mother hadn't. Sephy had already had one bombshell dropped on her today. She didn't need another.

'When was the last time you took the bike out for a ride?' Ethan asked, interrupting her thoughts.

Nora squinted a little against the watery winter sun. 'A while ago,' she said, her voice not much more than a whisper on the wind.

'I guess you've been too busy.'

Nora wrenched around to look at him but there was no sarcasm, no judgement. Only his quiet regard.

She found the response 'or something' on the tip of her tongue and wondered what it was about this man that had her keep admitting stuff.

They were silent for a while. Each soaking up the serene vista before them, until Ethan murmured, 'You know you're off the hook for helping set things up for Ryan. For one thing, I really don't need help. I'm quite capable of finding him a house and looking into new premises for Love Leisure myself.'

'Of course.' When her conscience snagged she chewed on the inside of her cheek. 'You did help me out when I really needed it, though. KPC only got the contract because of the way you pitched to Eleanor.' She turned her head to find his blue eyes darkening in a most fascinating way.

'I thought I made it clear. That was not about quid pro quo.'

'Still.' She thought about the embossed crisp white envelope with the Moorfield insignia and how it had been sitting on her desk at the office. She hadn't had to open it to know it contained two invitations to Eleanor's cocktail party.

'I would think that work is going to keep you too busy to keep coming down here to,' Ethan paused, 'help, anyway.'

'What about you? Will you be helping Ryan from Hull?'

'Ryan's closer to London, so I'll probably stay where I am. It's close enough to Heathstead for checking out locations.'

'I could help from London. Could find a way. Juggle some things around.'

'Delegate.'

Hackles rose. Feathers ruffled. 'I delegate. When it's appropriate. To be honest—'

'Oh, by all means, let's be honest.'

Nora hesitated and then channelled the last remnant of exhilaration from the bike ride. 'Well, if we were to be brutally honest, I find myself in need of your services, once again.'

'Services?' He cocked an eyebrow and her heartbeat pounded in her chest at the images flooding her imagination.

'Help,' she said on a dry swallow. 'I meant help,' she reiterated, wondering why on earth she was tethering herself to his company when she'd been trying to extricate herself from it. He mightn't like feeling that helping a person out meant helping them back in return, but she would sleep a lot better at night if she could ease the guilt and bury the temptation by helping him with Ryan.

'Of course.'

'Is that "of course—you know what I meant", or, "of course you'll help"?'

His warm blue eyes crinkled at the corners with more mischief. 'Why don't you tell me what you need?'

Lord. Why did everything that came out of his mouth make her feel so deliciously flirted with. 'Well, as you're going to be staying in London…Eleanor Moorfield has invited the two of us to a cocktail party she's hosting. It's a networking thing.'

'And you would like me to accept the invitation and take you as my—'

'Colleague,' she inserted lightning quick. 'Well, we don't have to go together per se, but if you could see your way to attending briefly, I know Eleanor would really appreciate it.'

'And it's important to keep the client happy.'

'Hey. I'm not suggesting you—'

'What?' he said with a grin.

Nora rolled her eyes. 'I'm definitely not suggesting you pimp yourself out. I'm simply asking if you could see your way to attending Eleanor's party.' She swiped her tongue over her lips. 'With me.'

'Okay then.'

'We wouldn't have to stay long,' she assured, using the tactic to persuade and then realising this would be the first real networking event she had attended since her father had died. Blinking she pushed away at the grief.

'What with you being so busy and all,' he teased.

'Exactly. Long enough for her to not think I'm rude. It would be more of an appearance thing, really—I, wait, you will?'

'I will.'

'Great. So I'll help you out with Ryan and you'll help me out with Eleanor—'

'—as it's important for your work.'

The way he stressed the last word had her scrabbling for composure. 'Speaking of work, I really ought to get back,' she said lamely.

'No rest for the wicked, huh?'

Again she searched his face and once again she could see nothing untoward to react to. But then he didn't look away and she was caught in the hypnotic beam of his baby-blues and the more he continued to stare, the surer she was that he could see right inside her. Right to the spot where the embers of all her risk-taking days lay buried.

With one lazy, clever, oh-so-sexy blink of his eyes he deliberately sparked those embers, and in doing so resurrected a flame that flared and took hold, so that she could feel herself heating up from the inside out.

Ethan's gaze dropped to her lips and Nora found herself swaying toward him, the flame inside her fanning out to lick over the top of the barriers she had put in place.

Sephy's words about acting before thinking rang in her ears like a permit to play, and with Ethan looking at her the way he was, how could she not think that he would make the best play-date ever?

And afterwards she'd—

Nora reared backwards. Afterwards, she'd what, exactly? She didn't have time to deal with a worst-case scenario outcome.

Dragging her gaze from his, she took one last glance out over the fields, determined to step off the path of temptation and back into the safe haven of numbness she'd been living in.

'You're right, no rest for the wicked.' She tried a smile to soften her words. Felt the knot inside her retighten reassuringly. 'I'll take us back to Sephy's and then I need to head back into London. Finish up some work that needs doing for Monday.'

'I don't suppose you can add in a couple more scenic miles on the return journey? The feel from my seat is quite breathtaking.'

'Don't you mean view?' She paused halfway to putting her helmet back on.

Ethan shifted on the seat so that as he moved to put on his helmet his chest brushed up against her back. 'No, I'm definitely focused on the feel.'

Nora shivered and felt a short, sharp tug on that knot inside of her as she surrendered an inch back into temptation. Flustered she shoved her helmet back on, snapped down the visor, started the bike and murmured, 'Better hold on tight, then.'

The ride back ended too soon, despite the fact that she had indeed added in a few extra miles. *Bad Nora!*

As she pulled to a stop inside the garage, she experienced the same crazy sense of anticipation that she had in the car with him the other day.

But as soon as there was no thrilling rush of speed and as soon as Ethan got off the bike, removing his glorious body heat, she was brought right down to earth and what-ifs and worst-case scenarios came raining down to mock her again.

With butterflies flitting about in her stomach as if she was sixteen again, she wheeled the bike back over to its usual place and walked over to the shelving unit to return her helmet. This time the fluffing of her hair was more to do with needing something to do while she tried to quell the anticipation.

She heard Ethan come up behind her and as he reached over to place his helmet on the shelving rack next to hers, his left hand rested on the shelf and she swallowed. He didn't speak, but took one more miniscule step closer and waited, as if for her reaction.

If he could see the physical reaction going on inside her he'd turn her around, slant his lips across hers and kiss her already. Fast. Hot. No time to think.

But no. Ethan's vice was patience, wasn't it? His other hand came up to slowly cage her in as he leant forward to remind her how he felt pressed up against her. Surrounding her. Teasing her. Tempting her.

There was only so much a girl could take. With heart galloping in her chest, she turned within the intimate cage of his arms to face him.

Ethan's blue eyes romanced her flushed face. 'I like what being out on that bike has done for you.'

Nora swallowed. *Move Nora. Because if you seriously think you can handle one taste of this gorgeous giant and then stop...* But it was as if she'd got friendly with the super-glue again: she was absolutely rooted to the spot.

'You look a little lighter.' He reached out and caught hold of a strand of her hair. 'A little freer.' Rubbed the flyaway strand slowly between the pads of his fingers as if memorizing the silky texture before tucking it tidily back behind her ear. His fingertips caressed the outer shell as he released the strand and her breath arrested in her throat. 'And you look a lot flushed,' he finished, his biceps bunching as he brought both hands up to drag the backs of his knuckles tenderly down the column of her throat, before sliding his hands back into her hair to hold her head. He redistributed his weight, widened his stance slightly to close the millimetre gap between them and she swallowed excitedly. Transfixed at what appeared to be his utter preparation to kiss her.

'I should probably not have ridden us so fast,' she said her breath finally coming out in a rush.

His eyes blazed white heat while his smile was gentle and did something to joggle that twisted mess of emotion inside of her. 'Speed-freak.'

'You say that as if it's a bad thing.'

'On the contrary. Fast can be good.'

'Exactly.' Nora nodded, unable to deny that she wanted to escape this any longer. Making his kiss happen in a rush of heat was what she would focus on to calm the swirling vortex of anticipation. 'There's nothing wrong with speed if it means you bypass the waiting,' she said, staring at his lips and willing him to lower his head.

Ethan chuckled and her gaze whipped up to meet his eyes. Damn it, there she was admitting stuff again. If he didn't shut her up with his lips, soon she'd be admitting to him how the sheer size of him when he was up this close and personal with her made her feel all… protected and…needy.

'But if all you ever do is rush to the end—don't you sometimes feel like you're missing out?'

'Missing out?' she frowned.

'Hmm.' Ethan lowered his head to nuzzle her hair away from her ear and whisper, 'Because sometimes slow can be good. Better even.'

Nora's eyes rolled back in her head at the combination of his words and the feel of his breath in her ear making her last-ditch cautious, 'Ethan, what are we doing?' come out on a distinct sigh.

'Oh, I think you know what we're doing.' His thumbs brushed the underside of her jaw as he tilted her head up. 'You do know, don't you, Nora?'

'Maybe.'

'And maybe you like. Maybe you want.'

'Maybe,' she managed to get out. Her hands came out to latch onto the hard wall of his chest. *Definitely*. She licked her lips. 'But—' What happened after? Her fingers clenched against his sweater. She needed to know. So she could prepare.

'No buts. Like I said; if I see something I want, I make sure I get it.'

'And it has to be slow like this,' she rushed out, her hand snaking under the heavy knit to get even closer. Closer to all that hot muscle.

Her breath blew out and landed against his throat making him shudder against her, but still he insisted, 'I kind of think it does. I want time to discover the secrets of your mouth.'

His lips hovered a millimetre above hers, intoxicating her, confusing her, mesmerising her.

'You going to give up those secrets for me, Nora?' he whispered.

'I—' She tried one last time to rally her thoughts. To stop the knot unravelling inside her. 'You say slow. I say fast. It's the same end result, you know.'

'It really isn't. Not when you want fast so you only have to feel fleetingly.'

'I—how..?'

He didn't let her finish. Instead his wonderfully sensual lips brushed slowly and reverently, over hers.

At the first instance of his touch Nora experienced a maelstrom of feeling pushing up from deep in her core.

It was insane that a barely-there kiss should ignite such depth of feeling that she felt instantly overwhelmed.

His lips left hers and she was suddenly, acutely, lost.

But then they lowered to hers again to press, to rub, to taste, and she felt anchored to him. Safe in the sensual storm he was creating.

Her fingers curled deliciously into the muscles of his abdomen as his teeth gently nipped at her bottom lip before sucking it into his mouth to salve with his tongue. She trembled as sensation after sensation came at her from all angles.

Moving her lips under his, she brought her tongue forward to slide against his, as if to offer her secrets wholly, wantonly. As if she knew he could be trusted with them.

At the first taste of him she whimpered, desperate not to taint him with the sadness that lay at her core.

It was too much.

And not fair on him.

Sudden and acute panic slammed into the wall of emotion rising up within her and splintered against the surface, so that she felt as if she was falling apart.

She couldn't do this. This wasn't fun—this was way more than fun. This was confusing and consuming and—

'Stop thinking,' Ethan whispered against her lips. 'Let go a little. I'll catch you.'

She wrenched her mouth from his. Her hand stopped plucking at the incredible solid ridges of his abs.

She stared up at him, breathing hard.

So he knew anyway.

Knew her dirty little secret—that she was fearful of all the emotion tied up in those knots inside her. That she was scared if she let go it would all tumble out uncontrollably and she'd look weak. As though she couldn't cope with her grief. With KPC. With her life.

Hot tears burned at the back of her eyes as the emotion bubbled out regardless. 'Seriously?' she husked. 'You'll catch me? You can't help yourself, can you—you want to save me? You want to rescue me?'

She watched as a dull flush formed across his cheekbones. Embarrassment thundered through her as it furiously set about tying back up all her ragged emotions with a pretty little bow.

'It couldn't be that I wanted to kiss you,' he said, his voice low, his jaw tight.

'Right,' she snorted. 'Kiss me better,' she asserted.

Ethan stepped back. Shoved his hands into his coat pockets.

'All that "I want to learn the secrets of your mouth…" Tell me you weren't trying to fathom me out and make me all better—to make yourself feel better.' If she wasn't so scared of the fact that he could see so easily right into her and see that she might need fixing, she might have wondered why he needed to feel better himself. She might even have wanted to help him feel better. Because she was drawn to him like no man she'd ever met. And that irritated the hell out of her. She didn't have the time. Couldn't spare the emotional energy. And now he was looking at her with a mixture of sympathy and anger.

'You know, I'm getting pretty tired of the way you keep judging me,' he said.

Nora searched his face. 'Because you don't like the shoe on the other foot or because my judgement is correct?'

Ethan held his hands up as if in surrender. 'Alright. Yes. I've seen what grief looks like when it's eating at a person. And the mask you try and hide it all behind? I've seen people adopt those too. And no, those masks don't quite conceal the fact that you don't know how to move forward. But, Nora, there is no right or wrong way to move forward when you're grieving.'

Nora blanched. 'You're wrong,' she spat out as his words had the panic escaping once more. There absolutely was a right way. And that way involved protecting everyone from having to witness it at all. Why shouldn't grief stay private? 'I have a responsibility to KPC. To keep the company running smoothly. Just because I refuse to curl up into a ball and—'

'But seeing all that in you is not why I kissed you, damn it,' Ethan said over her. 'I kissed you because I wanted to know if your lips would feel like I've been imagining they would, under mine. I kissed you because I wanted to explore the attraction between us. And I wanted you to open up, so that you'd be right there with me. *In* the experience. Not thinking. Not worrying. Not pushing your reaction to me back down inside to lie neglected, with everything else.'

Nora couldn't think straight. He couldn't just be content with this attraction between them. No, not Mr Knight-In-Shining-Armour, Ethan Love. He wanted more from her. He wanted to storm her defences and rip up her plan to keep out-running and out-distancing the wave of grief inside her.

But if work didn't see her through… If she took all her attention off KPC and gave *any* of it to Ethan, what would happen then?

Chapter Six

Nora's phone vibrated as it sat on top of her pile of papers.

She was not going to even glance at the incoming message.

She was going to get through this meeting in one mode: present; with her powers of concentration at optimum level. It was the very least her staff deserved.

At last the final member of senior staff started his update.

As he talked of penalty clauses and completion dates her gaze slid once more to her phone. Thankfully, the reflection from the overhead lights meant she couldn't see who it was who had left her a message.

As if she didn't know anyway.

She sniffed at her pathetic attempts to fool herself and her colleague paused in his presentation, obviously thinking she wanted to interject.

Nora waved her hand to indicate he should ignore her and carry on. She really hoped he hadn't said anything about the project that she needed to be aware of.

Damn Ethan to hell for dragging her out of her coma-like state.

Now she had all this anger roiling around inside her that she had to deal with. Although how she was supposed to do that when it sucked at her energy and left her feeling about as productive as a slug caught in a beer trap, she didn't know. Short of directing that anger at Ethan—and she really didn't feel like talking to him, what was she to do?

Of course, she was going to have to speak to him tonight. At the party.

But that was still hours away.

Hours.

Plenty of time to work out a coping strategy.

Abruptly she became aware that the room had lapsed into silence and as she glanced up from where her eyes had been glued to her phone she realised she'd been doing the one thing she had promised herself she wouldn't do today. Really, was it so hard to remain present during an important meeting? This was her company, for heaven's sake. Absolutely no more slacking-off, day-dreaming or thinking about Ethan bloody Love.

Gathering her wits and taking her cue from the fact that her colleague was now sitting down again, she smiled and said, 'Thanks Tim—everyone, it looks as if we're finishing the week in good shape.' No one looked as if she'd said anything out of place, so Tim's presentation hadn't thrown up anything she needed to worry about. She made a mental note to go over the minutes of the meeting anyway. She looked around at her team and felt a flood of guilt that she couldn't seem to get a handle on compartmentalising her life. Clearing her throat, she said, 'Before I call this meeting a wrap, I wanted to say how much I appreciate your extra efforts over the past few months. KPC is in a much healthier position than it was this time last year. The new services we've been introducing are beginning to carry us forward and I couldn't be happier with our progress.' She drew the pile of papers towards her in preparation for bringing the meeting to a close, glanced at her phone and turned it over so that she couldn't see the screen. 'If there's nothing else…Have a great weekend everyone.'

Vaguely she was aware that people were starting up conversations as they left the room in groups.

When most everyone had filed out, Nora flipped her phone over.

One message.

What was the betting it wasn't going to say: 'Sorry for calling you on your shit, because obviously I was grossly mistaken and you don't actually have any. At all.'

She tapped the screen to open the message and read: 'So if you still want me tonight, you're going to have to let me know. Ethan.'

He couldn't simply ask if they were still on for attending Eleanor's party that evening. She swore he spent actual time working out how to phrase things in a way that led her mind straight to sex. With him.

'Nora?'

Flustered, she looked up to find Tim standing in front of her. 'Sorry, Tim, did you have something you needed to add?'

'No. Well. I wanted to thank you for assigning me to the Moorfield account. It's a huge account and I appreciate your faith in me.'

'Not a problem. Is it Thursday that you're flying out to Italy to take a look at some of the property for us?'

'Yes. I'm looking forward to it.'

'I'm glad. Remember, if Eleanor wants to speak to me directly, it's not a reflection on your work—think of it as a little quirk of the client.'

'Okay. I was wondering if you could spare some time to take me through how you closed the deal. You know, talk me through what's not in the text books because I'd really appreciate the opportunity to learn.'

Nora's insides slopped and swirled as if someone had put her on a fast-spin washing cycle. The inescapable truth was that she hadn't earned the account herself. All she'd done in the end was the groundwork.

She wondered how Tim would react if he discovered that instead of the CEO of KPC getting the contract, she'd let someone from outside of the company pitch to Eleanor Moorfield and that possibly what had tipped the balance in KPC's favour was the scorching hotness of said stranger.

The excitement and positivity she'd got from announcing the account drained away.

Nora never used to doubt her ability to take KPC full steam ahead into the future. She had wanted to take what her father had built and improve upon it. Make him proud of her. She'd had all these ideas and dreams. But from the moment she'd found out her father was ill, to the hospital tests confirming he wasn't going to get better, she'd failed to adequately divide her focus and KPC hadn't got the best of her when it needed her most.

Jared had shown her she needed a hands-on approach in the new economy and the Moorfield account had been her first attempt at leading by example. Only it was Ethan, who wasn't even connected to the company, who had ridden in on a white horse to pitch the account and win it.

'The Moorfield account is what we needed,' Tim said. 'That's all I wanted to say, really. And that I'm enjoying working here again. Not that I wasn't before. It's that it feels as if things are turning around. I mean—' The poor man looked mortified.

'I understand what you meant, Tim.' It occurred to her that as the account manager, it was Tim she should have insisted on accompanying her to the party that evening. If she'd been thinking clearly she could have kept everything in-house and wouldn't have had to involve Ethan again.

She swore softly under her breath.

Ever since Ethan had wandered into her offices, thinking clearly had become a concept she was familiar with but apparently unable to adhere to.

Mentally she ran through her options. Should she see if she could inveigle a couple more invites for tonight? It would reinforce to Ethan that the evening was a strictly work thing. Except, she suspected, Eleanor's cocktail party wasn't designed to be about work. It wasn't being held for KPC. The cocktail party was merely an event where, if Nora networked successfully and subtly enough, she could make some more contacts for the company. Make up for the fact that she hadn't been the one to close the deal.

'If you're serious about next-level opportunity and broadening your knowledge base,' she told Tim, 'I'll have someone from sales involve you in the next pitch. I'm not saying no to me mentoring individual members of staff forever—only that I don't have time right now. Okay?'

'That would be great. Thanks, Nora.'

'No problem. I'm glad you're feeling so committed to KPC.' She gave him what she hoped was a warm and reassuring smile and then resumed gathering up her belongings.

When she heard the door close behind him she dropped her papers back onto the desk and leant her hands on the gleaming wooden surface for support.

If she didn't start wresting back control over her life she was going to lose KPC.

It was probably a good thing she would be the only person from KPC at the party tonight. That way she could start asserting that control. If her staff were there then they'd see her with Ethan. Eleanor already thought he was a member of her staff. If any of her actual staff realised that, they'd start thinking her personal life was getting mixed up in her work life.

The fact that it had already, and still was, was going to stop right now.

She picked up her phone to re-read Ethan's message.

'If you want me...'

Well, that was the first thing that was going to stop. All the wanting. She'd spend as short a time as possible with him this evening, and after that, any help she needed to provide with regards to getting Ryan settled once he left rehab she would conduct via email, or Skype or some other form of technology that meant she could put a little physical distance between them.

Nora pulled herself upright. What she needed in order to feel in better control this evening was a killer pair of shoes.

She brought her calendar up on her phone. She had a one-hour window mid-afternoon. She was going to go shoe shopping.

***

Ethan opened the shower door. Had someone knocked on his door? He waited a couple more seconds as steam billowed out around him. A brisk knocking sound made it to his ears. Shit. He was running late.

Shutting off the shower, he whipped a towel off the heated towel rack and wrapped it low on his hips as he padded out through the bathroom and across to the door.

What would have been a good idea, it turned out, was if as well as dragging on a towel, he had taken the time to drag extra air into his lungs, because as he opened the door and Nora King stood there staring back at him, he felt a definite lack of oxygen.

She appeared to be dressed in a black winter mac and, he swallowed as the blood drained from his head to travel south, a pair of sinfully sexy, black-satin, strappy high heels. She looked as if she'd walked straight out of an old-school fantasy and any minute was going to step over the threshold, untie the mac and drop it to reveal she was wearing nothing but the pair of shoes.

Her chocolate-brown eyes dilated as they drifted over him. Her lips parted slightly and, damn, but what red-blooded male wouldn't want a woman he was attracted to looking at him like she wanted to feast on him.

'You're not ready,' she said.

'I'm nearly ready,' he answered, wondering if she had the courage to lower her gaze further, because if she did, she was going to get an eye-full.

'You're not. You're all…wet,' she accused.

Christ. Her voice was laced with hunger. Was she deliberately trying to push him past his limit?

'You know, the longer you stand there staring, the longer it's

85

going to take me to get ready.'

He pushed the door open wide and waited for her to step inside. After what seemed like an age, she sauntered slowly past him, her hips swaying hypnotically. He chewed down hard on his tongue to stop it dropping out of his mouth and shut the door behind him.

Maybe he should have had her wait outside.

Her perfume was delicate, yet it burrowed under his skin and he realised he'd probably still be able to sense her in the air when he returned later that night. Alone.

Because the look on her face the other day, before she'd run out on him again, had made that fact more than clear.

She might want him.

But she wasn't going to let herself have him.

He watched as she stood in the centre of the room, her gaze now fixed on the unmade bed and instead of thinking about writhing limbs—his and hers—he found himself embarrassed.

It really shouldn't matter that he'd fallen asleep in the middle of the afternoon. He tried telling himself that his body needed the rest and to hell with trying to keep to a regular sleeping pattern to break the cycle of insomnia. He knew that he was never going to be allowed to go back to working in aid response if he couldn't trust in his ability to store his energy by sleeping at the drop of a hat, but something about Nora and her silent judgement made him hate being the guy with question marks hanging over his ability to do a good job.

He scrubbed a hand over his face. The problem now was that he'd spent so long not sleeping since Italy that getting a few uninterrupted hours had left him feeling completely off-kilter.

The shower hadn't helped as much as he'd needed it to. He wondered if he'd get away with going back under the spray, only this time, turning the temperature to ice-cold. Probably not, if the fact that Nora's eyes now kept darting from the bed to the bathroom door meant anything.

'Perhaps I'll wait for you downstairs in the bar,' she told him, throwing him more off-balance with her new clipped tone. 'I appear to have interrupted something.'

Ethan tried to get his head in gear. Nora pulled on the belt of her coat as if to tighten it further before attempting to stride past him. His hand shot out to latch onto her arm and bring her around to face him, so that he could see eyes that shone equally with bruised hurt and spiced fury. Wait a bloody minute, there was absolutely no way she could be thinking... 'You really think I have a woman stashed in the bathroom?' He wanted to shake her, because from the look on her face she was thinking exactly that. His chest puffed with indignation. 'Yes, Nora, because obviously I can't cope with any form of rejection and so as soon as you ran out on me again last week I came straight back here and found a willing female.'

She had the grace to drop her accusing gaze as the colour wended its way over her face.

'Ethan.' His name left her lips on a mortified moan. 'I'm sorry. I—'

'Can't stop thinking the worst of me? Well, I need you to try because it's getting really boring, really fast.'

She looked up at him as if she couldn't understand why he would bother giving her a second, third and fourth chance to break her bad habit and he found himself wondering who in her life hadn't given her those extra chances. Had expectations been so ridiculously high, growing up in the King family? Was that why she found it so difficult to show anyone something other than complete control over her feelings?

'I apologise,' she said in a formal tone. 'It's none of my business what you get up to. It's not as if you and I—'

He really had no idea why he found her so adorable when she babbled, but as she dug herself deeper and deeper he knew he had to take pity on her. The instant his hand settled on her cheek, she stilled. 'Look, let's try this again, shall we? I'm sorry I'm running late, but I can get ready in five minutes flat. Now do you want to wait up here or would you prefer to wait downstairs?'

'I—' she licked her lips and it took everything inside him not to drop his mouth down onto hers and do the same. 'I guess I'll wait up here.' She took one step away from him, then another, turned around and grabbed the TV remote. 'I'll watch a bit of TV or something.'

'You do that,' he agreed and walked over to the wardrobe to get his tux. 'I'll get changed in the bathroom.'

Could one actually die from mortification? The question continued to vex Nora as she stared at the television screen, feigning utter absorption. For good measure, she turned up the volume to muffle any potential calls for assistance from the bathroom.

She didn't understand.

She had done 'the shopping of the shoes'.

Usually when she found the perfect pair that made her feel confident and in control, what happened next was that she actually felt confident and in control.

All the way to the hotel she had felt calm and composed.

Convinced she had the ability to remain friendly and not flirty.

Convinced she could stop all the wanting of him.

Her hands clenched around the remote control in her lap. The problem was that now she associated Ethan with shoes—with his choosing of them for her.

So that what had slammed into her when he'd opened the door, apart from the surge of heat at seeing that glorious body of his, was the absolute realisation that she'd chosen the shoes she was wearing, not with remaining in control in mind, but more specifically, with him in mind. With how he might think she looked in them.

And then, to lay bare to him how enslaved she was, she'd taken one look at the rumpled sheets on the huge unmade bed and given voice to the completely unfounded jealousy bubbling away inside her.

She was tempted to raid his mini-bar for alcohol and down a bottle or two to take the edge off the hot needles of stinging humiliation. Knowing her luck, though, she'd get a little too tipsy, forget her ground rules for the evening and throw herself at him.

So instead she stared at the television screen and tried to calm down. Everything would be better once they were at the party. Amongst people who could distract her from the grip of this ridiculous physical attraction.

The bathroom door opened and she turned automatically.

Mercy.

Ethan in a tux was like having a living, breathing, license-to-thrill James Bond at her service.

Her eyes tracked him like prey as he wandered over to the nightstand to pick up his wallet, phone and keys, and slip them into his trouser pockets.

Why was it she had forbidden herself to jump his bones again?

Oh, yeah.

It was because of all the feelings. Feelings he brought out in her. Strong feelings that she would rather go on keeping buried, so that she could get on with general everyday business.

Huh.

Not for petty reasons, then, but for self-preservation.

She switched the television off and then reached for her clutch bag and opened it. 'Here, this is for you,' she said as she drew out a piece of black material and tossed it gently in his direction.

Ethan caught it automatically and held it up for inspection. 'You brought me a bowtie?' he asked with a hint of a smile on his lips.

'I figured it was best to come prepared,' she replied, aiming for friendly not flirty.

'You know, you can't prepare for everything in life,' Ethan mused.

Tell me something I don't know.

Nothing had prepared her for watching her father battle cancer. And nothing on earth could have prepared her for the cancer winning. He was the strongest man she ever knew…but even with all of them, all the stubborn Kings in battle alongside him, they had fought the fight and lost.

'I couldn't wear one of those?' he asked, looking behind her right shoulder, snapping her, thankfully, out of her reverie.

Nora turned to find the vase of ties she'd gifted him the day he'd won the Moorfield account sitting on his dressing table. She stared at the colourful display, not caring if Ethan's distraction had been deliberate or not, only pleased that she had thought about the cancer and managed to contain the rage.

She swung back to him. 'Might be a little too fashion-forward for this evening.'

'Well, you're going to have to tie this on me, then. I have no idea how to.'

Blood pumped heavily through Nora's veins. Putting it on him, being so close, would be like a test. A test that, if she passed, would be a sign that she could be in his company and not feel overpowered by the strength of her desire. Walking up to him, she took the bowtie out of his hands and then reached her arms up high to flick up the collar of his shirt. Her fingers brushed into his hairline and she forbade herself to let them linger or slide in deeper. She had a lot riding on her passing the test. Avoiding potential meltdown was a pretty huge prize.

She clenched her teeth and tried not to breathe in how good he smelled.

Her knuckle brushed against his Adam's apple as she fastened the top button of his collar. He breathed in sharply and her fingers shook a little in acknowledgment of his reaction to her touch.

Concentrate, Nora, concentrate.

Disassociate or something.

'So do they pull you aside in private school and teach you all how to tie bowties?' Ethan's deep voice whispered over her as she passed one end of the material through the loop she'd created.

Grief, sudden and brutal, rolled over her in a wave. Disassociation achieved.

Her fingers faltered.

Her insides scrambled.

She would not cry.

It would be really stupid to cry over a bowtie.

Ethan didn't touch her, but she could feel the concern flowing from him. 'Nora? What did I say?'

She shook her head, sniffed and squared her shoulders. She should thank him, really. At least she wasn't thinking about him and all his sexiness now.

Raising her head, she pasted a smile on her face and blinked to clear her over-bright eyes. 'Nothing. I'm being silly.' Her eyes dropped back to the bowtie because if she saw sympathy in his eyes the teardrops trembling on her lashes would definitely spill over. She cleared her throat, hoping to eject the wobble. 'My father taught me to tie bowties. Took me ages to get the hang of them. Thinking about it, he probably got mother to re-tie them before they got to whichever function they were going to.' With adult perspective, the sudden sweet suspicion her father might have done that to spare her feelings brought the sadness even closer, forcing her to acknowledge how scared she was of the giant ache inside her that threatened a bottomless depth.

Ethan's hand came up to squeeze against hers reassuringly before dropping back to his side. 'That's a nice father-daughter memory to have.'

'It is.' She sniffed again, wanting desperately for the warm memories to stay at surface level. Not overtake and overwhelm and feel so raw that his passing felt like it had happened yesterday.

'You're lucky to have been so close to him.'

Her fingers tugged on the ends of the bowtie to straighten it. She was. She knew that absolutely. Knew also that they'd been close because she hadn't let up. She'd taken her hero-worship and the streak of stubbornness that ran through all the Kings and applied herself to not becoming the invisible middle child.

'Are you close to your parents?' she asked, curiosity about him getting the better of her as she fiddled with the ends of the bowtie.

'No,' he answered with steely inflection.

Well that was succinct. Nora frowned. 'Do they know what you're doing for Ryan?'

'Yes.'

'And they're not interested?'

'My parents operate on the strongest of beliefs that if you throw enough money at a problem it disappears so that depends on whether you count receiving a cheque in the post to cover the cost of Ryan's treatment as interested.'

'I would not, no.' She swept her gaze up to meet his flashing blue eyes and for a split second she worried he didn't believe her. 'They're not close with Ryan either?' she asked.

'Not really.'

Nora knew that both Jared and Sephy had, in different ways, been through the wringer with their father. She hadn't because she'd been powerfully interested in the one thing that interested him above everything. KPC. But their mother had been there equally for her three children. None of them had ever felt a complete lack of parental love.

'So what are your parents interested in, if not their children's welfare?'

'It's not that they're totally disinterested,' he said coming to their defence—a reaction she understood and appreciated because you could say what you liked about your family, but if anyone else said anything about them… 'It's more that they find it easier to spend money on a problem rather than personal time and effort. Now that dad's retired, time and effort is reserved for sailing around the world on their yacht and visiting friends.'

Wow. So seeing how that chip on his shoulder had formed. If his parents' parenting style was more from the cold and clinical end of the spectrum, was that why he spent all his time helping others? To set himself aside from his parent's selfishness?

She thought about what he was doing for his brother. How he'd given his help so generously when she had needed it. For someone to have been brought up in such a cold, money-oriented household, he sure had warmth and compassion in spades.

Her hands dropped away from his bowtie. From him.

'Finished,' she said, softly.

'Thanks. You okay?'

She nodded, feeling the last tendrils of loss tickle across her as they drifted away. They would wrap themselves around her again no doubt, but hopefully not tonight. 'Do me a favour, though?' she said staring up at him. 'Don't be too nice to me. It took ages to do my makeup and we really haven't got time for me to re-do it.'

'Got you. Shall we, then?'

'Sure.' She bent to the bed to retrieve her clutch and glanced up as he quietly called her name. 'Yes?' she prompted when he looked as if he was weighing up whether to tell her what was on his mind or not.

Ethan stared down at the bed briefly. 'The bed is unmade because I fell asleep earlier. I'm not sleeping regularly since—well, for a while now. I have a little insomnia.'

Nora knew it must have cost him to tell her. In the short time she had known him he had appeared an effective thoroughly chilled-out master over every facet of his life. Apart from when he'd been staring at the TV news report on the earthquake, she realised. What had he experienced to stop him sleeping? 'Okay.' She searched for a way of keeping things light so that they could meet in the middle of this new being-friendly-with-each-other. 'Well. Consider that tonight, if the event turns out to be really boring, you might get the chance to drop off again.'

He laughed that laugh that coated her insides like warm melted butter and put his hand at the small of her back to steer her out the room and down the corridor.

So this was what being friendly as opposed to flirty with him felt like.

Nora felt the heat from his hand in the small of her back and tried not to compare it to how similar it felt to still being completely and utterly attracted to him.

Chapter Seven

'So I have a few ground rules before we go in,' Nora said as the car pulled up outside the Mayfair venue for the evening's party.

'Ground rules?' Ethan smirked as he got out of the car and came round to take the door from the chauffeur and hold it open for her. 'Your dates usually go for a bit of that, do they?'

She looked up at him. 'This is not a date.'

'You could always change your mind about that,' he said, sweeping his gaze over her, thinking that if it *was* a date, he'd let her strike sparks off him all evening to enjoy seeing the fire flash in her eyes.

'I prefer to keep this as agreed. A work-slash-you-helping-me-out thing.'

'Well, whatever this is,' he said, leaning in close, 'I'm more of a make-it-up-as-we-go-along kind of guy.'

'And they encourage that attitude in your line of work, do they?' she asked, with a delicate arching eyebrow.

Ethan held himself rigid as the reel of events surrounding Pietro's rescue unfolded in his head. Guilt rushed in, found its target and landed a swift left-hook. 'You think if I disregarded a rule, that I wouldn't have a damn good reason for doing so? You think I'd wade in without due care?'

'No, no, of course not. I'm sorry.' She laid her hand on his forearm, confusion and concern etched across her delicate features. 'What happened in Italy, Ethan?'

He shouldn't have told her about the insomnia. Now she thought she knew all about him. 'Nothing. Nothing at all.'

'But if you can't sleep because of it—'

'I'm fine. I overreacted. I'm sorry,' he said, taking care to shut the car door rather than slam it. He didn't know how, but somehow her good opinion of him had started to matter a little too much. But then, he'd probably do better at dealing with *that* if he stopped reacting as if every look or comment held an accusation behind it.

Together they walked up to the spotlit building before them. 'This is nice,' he said inanely, forcing all the endless questions he asked himself about *that day* back into the box in his head marked 'Ethan's Archives'. Getting het up about the outcome of that report wasn't going to change anything. He'd given his statement. All he had to do now was start sleeping better and keep himself busy until the verdict was in.

Okay, so he wasn't doing great at the sleeping part, but the keeping busy part?

He'd been doing all right at that.

Or maybe it was time to admit he'd been fooling himself into thinking that.

He'd been doing very little to keep himself stretched and busy because a certain brown-eyed princess kept stealing into his thoughts day and night, making him lose track, making him daydream, making him want…more than he should and certainly more than he had time for.

As soon as he'd set things up for Ryan, he would be going back to the site of the earthquake in northern Italy. The community would still need help and he had to trust in the system. Trust he would be allowed back to his job. So that he could keep the promise he'd made to that little boy. He pinched the bridge of his nose as he thought about how slowly time passed when you were small and how it felt the first time you were let down by an adult.

He didn't want to be that person for Pietro.

'This building used to be a church,' Nora was babbling. 'It hadn't been used for decades until, a couple of years ago, three multi-millionaires decided to buy it and turn it into something usable again. It's *the* place to host events at the moment.' Just before they reached the entrance, Nora pulled him to one side. 'Um, yeah—so the ground rules for tonight. Mostly, I'm thinking no touching.'

'I'm not allowed to touch anything?' He raised his hands for inspection, frowning slightly when he realised the large gash he'd sustained to his left palm getting Pietro out of that building hadn't completely healed. He caught Nora focusing on his hands, and wanting to believe she hadn't seen the evidence of his recent escapade, he closed his fists. 'These hands not refined enough for you? I realise they're more used to building shelter and handing out food packs, but I can assure you, they know how to be gentle.'

Nora cleared her throat. 'Actually, I meant me—no touching me.'

His head tipped to the side as he considered her words. How was it that she said no touching her and now that was all he wanted to do, for hours and hours. She made him want to break every rule she laid down, which, considering he was currently suffering the consequences of breaking rules, meant he shouldn't even be interested and yet... He felt the twinkle forming in his eye. 'No touching, huh? But what if there's dancing?'

'There will be no dancing.'

His smile built. 'What if I pass you a drink and our fingers accidentally touch?'

'I'm quite capable of getting my own drink.'

'What if I need to step between you and a lecherous old fart?'

The glint in her brown eyes became steely. 'Because I haven't made it clear already that I don't need rescuing?' She didn't let him make a comeback. Instead she drew breath deep into her lungs and said, 'Look, what sort of impression do you think Eleanor is going to form if she sees you—'

'Sees me, what?' He didn't think his grin could get any wider.

97

'You know. Getting all touchy-feely with me.'

'To be honest, I'm having more fun hearing the words "touchy-feely" come out of your mouth to care much about what Eleanor Moorfield might think.'

Her chin tilted in a magnificent display of haughtiness.

'Did you know you get this little wrinkle, right here,' unable to help himself he touched the bridge of his nose, 'when you're mad.'

'I'm glad you at least recognise I'm annoyed, because it means you have some idea of how it could damage KPC's reputation if its staff are seen acting inappropriately.'

'But Eleanor Moorfield already knows I don't work for KPC.'

'I'm not even going to go into how it's then going to look when she discovers you don't even work for—' The wrinkle in her nose met and merged delightfully with a frown. 'Wait—what do you mean she already knows?'

He braced himself. 'Tell me you didn't really think I was going to start your pitch with a lie.'

She stared at him dumbfounded.

'It would have been totally unethical. God, you should see your face. Do you always assume the worst of me because you're nervous around me, or do you genuinely expect me to behave in a socially uneducated manner, wherever I am?'

'I'm not nervous around you. Why would I be nervous around you?'

'So the babbling, foot-tapping, constantly thinking I'm going to act crazy, stuff comes from..?'

She looked at him as if he was in no way special, which might have stung except he reminded himself he didn't need to be affected by what she thought of him.

'So what did you tell her?' she asked.

'I apologised and told her I was a family friend who was helping out while you dealt with an emergency.'

'But I don't understand. If Eleanor knew you didn't work for KPC, why did she make it so obvious she wanted you here tonight?'

Nora brought a hand to her lips. 'Oh.'

'What do you mean, "oh"?'

Her fingers dropped away from her mouth, leaving a huge smile on her face. 'I think maybe she might have insisted I invite you for more personal reasons.'

'That's ridiculous,' he said knowing there had been absolutely no blurring of the lines in that meeting.

'Is it?' she deadpanned. 'Could it be that you turned on a little too much charm during your pitch?'

Great. Ethan ground his teeth together. One more black mark against him. 'I was completely appropriate and respectful.'

'I don't know, Ethan, maybe you're so irresistible that she couldn't help herself. I mean, aren't you the man who guaranteed me she'd be impressed with you. You even gave me the cocky attitude to go with it.'

'I did not.'

'You did. You were all,' she stepped back lowered her voice, puffed out her chest and said, "What do you think, brush up as well as the next guy?" And I said "You'll do" and you said—'

'All right, all right—I know what I said.' He ran a hand over the back of his hair. He sneaked a look at her and realised with a start that she was taking him out for a spin.

Nora King was loosening the straight-jacket enough to play with him? Payback was an absolute necessity. 'Well, I certainly don't want to embarrass her at her own party if that's what she thinks. We'll have to make sure she gets the message that it's not on the cards. She knows we don't work together—that we're friends. You'll have to help me give her the impression we're way more than friends.' He leant forward and whispered in her ear, 'It might involve you…touching me.' He grinned against her cheek when he felt her breath escape in a rush. 'We should start now. Get a little warmed up before we face her. I'll give you a breakdown of exactly where you should touch me and the look in your eyes as you do—' He broke off, laughing when Nora punched him not so lightly on the arm.

'You are—'

'Irresistible. So you said. Don't worry. I'll try not to let it go to my head.'

'—such a pain, is what I was going to say.' Her hand came out to tuck a loose strand of hair behind her ear. She bit her lip and then looked away as if to gather herself.

'What is it?'

'Nothing. Okay, it's something—a tiny thing,' she shrugged as if that would make her thoughts form into some sort of order, 'this is the first event like this I've attended since—' she ran out of words and his heart went out to her. 'I'm sorry I don't know what I'm trying to say, really.'

'You're trying to say that nothing feels easy since your father passed away. One minute you want to be here, the next you're wondering why you accepted the invitation.'

The relief on her face made him want to touch her. Run his fingertips softly over her face and erase all the worry she clung too so religiously because she was afraid if she let it go she wouldn't be able to control it. But she'd said no touching. 'It's a party. Let's keep it that simple. The minute it isn't, you say, and we leave.'

'Thank you. I—'

Now the touching was imperative. He reached out and pressed a finger gently against her lips to stem the gratitude he didn't want her regretting releasing later. 'Come on. Let's go in.'

They joined the queue that had formed and Nora busied herself retrieving the invitations from her bag to pass to the security men checking them against the guest list at the entrance.

Once inside, Ethan looked around, trying to keep the slightly stunned expression from showing on his face. The old church flagstone floor was lit to resemble a carpet of fresh green grass, complete with daisies springing up in clumps. The stone pillars had flower bowers projected onto them from clever lighting.

Trees filled the lobby, their branches dripping with crystal birds

100

and butterflies. Strings of pearls in golds, pinks, lilacs and powdery-blue hues hung in ropes linking each tree together.

'Er, you might have mentioned we were expected to fall down the rabbit-hole tonight.' He blinked, bizarrely fascinated by a life-sized deer peering out at him from between two pillars.

'It's supposed to be a forest coming to life. Isn't it fabulous? I'm going to check my coat.'

'I'll come with you,' he muttered, worried he was going to start seeing hares jumping at his feet or something. 'You know there could have been another reason Eleanor played you like she did,' he said as they waited.

Nora turned from her space in the line to look at him. He shrugged his shoulders nonchalantly and said, 'Maybe she saw something in the way I enjoyed taking my time to choose those shoes for you and thought she'd do a little match-making.'

Nora's hands paused in their untying of her coat belt. 'You know, already you're not helping to make this feel simple.'

'It's feeling fun though, right?' he teased back.

She eyed him a little suspiciously. 'I'll get back to you on that.' Removing her coat, she handed it over to the assistant at the desk.

'You worry too much about things you can't control,' he quipped.

'Yeah? You worry too much about what people think about you.'

He opened his mouth to tell her in no uncertain terms that he absolutely did not, but his brain finally caught up with what his eyes were relaying. She was a vision in red. The low whistle left his lips without conscious thought. 'By the way, the way you looked at me when I opened my hotel room door earlier? Well, right back at you.'

Her mouth dropped open as she turned to look at him, completely missing the fact that the assistant behind the coat check desk was holding a ticket out for her.

Ethan reached over and took the ticket and placed it in his jacket pocket. He needed something to do with his hands or he was going to break her rule again before they'd even got inside the party proper. 'What?' he said as his eyes skated over the scarlet satin cocktail dress that clung in all the right places and made him want to tango with her. And other things. Lots of other things. 'You said no touching. You didn't say anything about no complimenting.'

She got the 'v' in the centre of her forehead that made him itch to reach out and smooth his thumb over it.

'You-I-You—'

'Uh-huh.' He nodded in understanding and then, out of the side of his mouth added, 'I think we're holding up the queue.' He held his hand out for her so that she had no choice but to place hers in his and allow herself to be led through another set of doors and on into the main area of the party.

As Ethan's eyes adjusted to the ongoing forest-in-spring theme, he tried not to think about how he wasn't in Kansas any more or how much money it cost to put on a party like this and how that money could be better spent. The thing was he did know how much it cost to put parties like this together. His parents had spent lots of money on entertaining over the years—the bigger the party, the better and more perfect their life was. He had been glad he'd left that life behind.

In many ways life was simpler on deployment. Providing the basics in life was a great leveller. But Ethan knew he had to be able to walk in both worlds. For Love Leisure to allow him capital to volunteer it had needed to operate smoothly in the luxury end of the market. Coming from money had meant it wasn't much of a transmission and over time he'd learned to square the circle.

Mostly.

A live swing band had Sinatra'd-up some modern hit songs. Waiters and waitresses dressed as woodland sprites and nymphs passed around canapés and cocktails. Giant tree stumps served as tables and chairs.

Eleanor Moorfield sashayed into his sightline and smiled. Her eyes drifted to Nora standing beside him and her smile grew

like hell for her to acknowledge with words rather than looks that it could be more. Already was more.

'You know I really ought to start mingling,' she responded with an exaggerated look around her.

'Okay.' He dumped his plate on a passing waiter's tray, his hand then free to run a finger around the collar of his shirt. 'I guess,' he searched the room for something to anchor his thoughts to and was surprised when his gaze swung back to hers and found it there in the genuine and uncomplicated interest shining in her eyes, 'it began with how much my father's job required us to move around when we were growing up. Ryan and I were always the new kids. I think I wanted to find something that remained the same wherever I was, so I started volunteering at local aid charities and started fundraising. I kept getting taller and taller and one university holiday someone at the charity suggested I got out to Africa with them and put my size to good use—helping the team build a new school. I loved it. Loved getting stuck in. Loved the teamwork. Loved the looks on those kids' faces when they got their school. By the time I was halfway through university I'd been working for the charity every holiday, mostly doing admin but sometimes getting to travel out to where they were and help. Because I'd lived in or visited so many different places growing up I wasn't easily spooked in new environments. I liked making a difference and I wanted to do more.'

'And did they let you do more?'

He smiled, remembering how he'd assumed he'd walk straight into a job as a response- team member. He'd had to learn pretty quickly that the charity wasn't there to provide him with an outlet to make himself feel better. It was there to help others who couldn't help themselves. 'Not until I'd built up some useful experience in the world of work and completed a lot more training programmes.'

'Have you seen any conflict?' she asked and he knew she was simply interested in his work but they were definitely straying into an area he didn't want to get into. He had enough bad memories of Italy without having to revisit the one's he *never* let himself think about.

'Yes…Syria, and no, I'm not talking about that.'

'Ever? Or because we're at a party?'

'Because we're at a party,' he answered, surprising the both of them. Huh. For a woman who babbled a lot, got nervous a lot and was afraid of her own emotions, she did have this quiet, simple, soothing way of getting him to talk.

She popped another canapé into her mouth. 'Where does Love Leisure fit into all of this?'

He shrugged. 'I needed a business I could build that would make enough profit to fund becoming a response team member and give me useful experience. Management experience that I could take into the field.'

She shook her head in wonder. 'You must have had to work so hard to avoid all those new business pitfalls. Do you hold any passion for Love Leisure or could it have been any business?'

'Will it disappoint you terribly to know that it isn't what gets me out of bed in the morning?'

'No—not terribly. Maybe if you didn't have your other work…'

'What would you be doing if you didn't have KPC?'

Nora blinked. Something soft drifted across her face and was instantly chased away. 'I can't think of anything I'd rather be doing.'

Well, hell. Here they were, he thought, getting along famously. Doing the new friendship thing and talking about themselves, revealing things about themselves…and he was fairly convinced she had just lied to him.

As if she realised what she'd done, she said, 'Speaking of KPC—'

He was tempted to push but she'd already given more of herself tonight than he thought he'd get, so he eased them both back to safer ground. The last thing he needed was to get into a little quid pro quo, secret fear-sharing conversation. 'We weren't talking about you deciding to dance with me?' he asked completely changing the subject.

She smiled and her eyes drifted momentarily over the couples on the dance floor. 'Nice try.'

He blew out the breath he'd been holding. The night was still young. He'd get her to change her mind before they left.

Nora smiled distractedly as the company executive from a chain of ready-to-wear fashion said goodbye and walked over to join another group of guests. She sincerely hoped her subtle sales pitch had made sense. It was difficult to tell when all her energy was focused on Ethan, who was this very minute on the other side of the large room, chatting with a stunning petite woman in an eye-watering tight-green dress.

As the woman dazzled and smiled up at him, and jealousy nipped at Nora's ankles before working its way up, she couldn't help feeling that if she went over and joined them, the combined vision of her in her red dress and the woman in her green dress would give Ethan the perfect representation of 'stop' and 'go'.

She frowned because deep down she hadn't worn the red dress to reinforce her decision to stop wanting Ethan. She'd worn it because she looked good in it. And hadn't she wanted Ethan to think that too?

Shaking her head at herself, Nora took a sip from the glass of champagne she'd been nursing for the last thirty minutes and deliberately looked in the opposite direction as she made her way slowly along the edge of the crowded dance floor, skirting between the couples dancing and the pockets of guests chatting.

What she needed to do was give herself a little pep talk. So far this evening she had coped with the fact that this was the first party she'd attended since her father had died and she hadn't crumbled. She'd even managed to give out a few business cards and make a few sales pitches. And if it all seemed a little more like hard work than usual, well that was understandable, wasn't it? The main thing was that she was here, networking and representing KPC. It no longer mattered that it was Ethan who was responsible for her being here. It was KPC that was actually doing the work for Eleanor and so far the shoe designer hadn't given her any impression she wasn't happy with what KPC had come up with for her.

Nora turned her head, her eyes seeking out Ethan again as she admitted to herself that the greater pull of the evening wasn't the business contacts she could make, but how she could work herself into a secluded corner with him and listen to him talk some more about his work. She wanted to find out what had happened on his last job to make him unable to sleep properly. Find out what happened in his family for his brother to go one way and he in another. Find out about him so that she could get a handle on why he fascinated her, because it wasn't simply that he flirted so well and looked so good.

Although, my, but he did flirt well and he did look *so* good. Like filings drawn to a magnet, she spotted him, eyes widening when she caught him looking straight back at her. Her heart tripped over itself, nearly winding her in the process. She had been able to see him out of the corner of her eye wherever she was in the room. As if whenever she moved, he then deliberately moved into her orbit. Proper knight-in-shining-armour behaviour, standing there ready to rescue. Or was it simply that he didn't want her to forget who she had come with? Like she could forget when every move he made seemed to find its way into her consciousness.

She needed to remember Ethan was in her life *temporarily*. KPC was for life. But then he smiled and she smiled right back and promptly collided with someone because she wasn't looking where she was going.

'I'm so sorry,' she said to the person she'd bumped into as hands shot out to grasp her arms and steady her.

'No damage done. It's Leonora isn't it, Leonora King?'

'Yes. I—' Nora searched for a name to put to the face of the sixtyish-year-old man standing in front of her. She used to be better at this. Used to be the person who supplied the names to her father as he moved around at a function, networking.

'We haven't formally met,' said the man holding out his hand. 'Tod Collingsworth. I knew your father.'

'Of course,' she smiled, shook his hand and prayed he didn't say anything about her father that would have the knot of grief rising to the surface.

'I understand Eleanor has signed a very nice deal with KPC. Congratulations.'

'Thank you.' Suddenly the industry he was from clicked with her and her business instincts kicked right in, and it was as if she'd been doing this for years again. 'I've heard that the new shopping complex on Oxford Street is turning into a bit of a white elephant. Seems to me they need to bring their rates down in line with the current market or none of the major retailers will lease the remaining space and footfall is going to drop to non-existent,' she paused for effect. 'Still happy to have your flagship store there?'

Tod Collingsworth grinned. 'Well, now that you mention it. Lease comes up for renewal soon.'

Nora grinned back, feeling the fire in her belly for the first time in months. 'Then now would seem like the best time to be thinking about whether you need increased floor space, or whether you need less space but a better, more accessible, location, with a targeted and loyal footfall.'

'Perhaps I should stop by KPC next week and go through some options?'

'Absolutely. I'll have my assistant call you to set something up.' Nora's grin got bigger. She'd been worried she'd let herself become so blindsided by Ethan that the one thing she thought she could always rely on whenever tough times came to call—her love of business, her love for *her* business, KPC, paled suddenly in comparison.

But KPC was going to land Tod Collingsworth as a client. She could feel it in her bones. Hard work and networking. This was what she needed to keep doing to survive this last year and get her passion and drive back.

'And when will Jared be joining KPC on a more permanent basis,' Tod asked, completely flooring her.

'Jared?' Nora felt slightly nauseous as a flutter of panic beat beneath her breastbone. One minute she'd been back where she loved, talking business and feeling confident. The next…

'Your brother, Jared. I had heard that he had been working at KPC while your father underwent treatment?'Nora made herself stand taller, lengthening her spine to compensate for feeling as if someone had let all the air out of her. Is this what everyone who knew her father really thought now? That she was only some sort of caretaker manager? Not good enough at her job for forever? 'Jared came over to consult on one particular project under my management,' she forced out, hardly able to tell a potential client KPC had been struggling. 'That time coincided with my father's illness, but Jared was never going to re-locate back here. He has his own business. As I have KPC.'

With renewed vigour she tried to hold onto the last of the confidence she had won back. The confidence that had been such a part of the old her. 'I do hope the fact that Jared won't be coming back to KPC hasn't put you off coming in to see us next week?'

'No of course not,' Tod Collingsworth was quick to answer. 'Like I said, I knew your father and I'm sure he knew what he was doing when he promoted you, eh?'

'I'm sure he did,' she bit out, her smile frozen in place. 'Although he's no longer around to ask, is he?'

A fact that made her so stupendously angry at him. There were times, like now, when she could barely draw breath.

Chapter Eight

Oh please, please tell me those words didn't actually leave my lips?
Nora stood floundering in front of Tod Collingsworth, watching
in horror as he turned beetroot-red. Oh, they had—they had left
her lips. The room pressed in on her, the lights now too harsh
and the music too invasive as she tried and failed miserably to
form a sentence that could somehow take away from her unfor-
giveable rudeness.

Then, as if someone had called for help from an interpreter,
Ethan appeared at her side. His face was a picture of calm concern
and she wanted to throw back her head and howl at the unfairness
of it all because why should it be *him* that understood.

Ethan nudged her elbow gently and when he got her attention,
stared pointedly at her drink before raising his gaze back to hers.
Belatedly she realised that he was silently telling her to sip from
the glass and with a jerky movement she lifted the crystal to her
lips and drank to try and ease the tightness in her throat.

Anger at her father dying on her, anger at her second-guessing
herself buzzed through her nervous system and if she didn't get a
handle on it she was either going to combust or have no control
over it oozing out through her pores and infecting innocent people.
Like it had poor Mr Tod Collingsworth.

Scrabbling to shove the anger back into the black hole inside

111

herself, she vaguely became aware that Ethan was introducing himself to her father's old friend and chatting about Love Leisure. Very deliberately and very helpfully he was giving her time to pull herself together.

A confident and easy social grace emanated from him, but she forgot to be jealous of those qualities. Instead, as she allowed his deep voice to penetrate the choke-hold on her emotion, her brain started to clear so that when there was a natural lull in the conversation she found she was able to step forward, lay her hand softly on Tod Collingsworth's sleeve and with her voice low and somewhat shaky say, 'Mr Collingsworth, I would like to apologise. I didn't intend to sound so flippant. I wouldn't want you to think—'

'Of course not,' he rushed to say. 'Please don't think that I meant to imply—what I want to say is that you're quite obviously steering KPC in the right direction. I happen to know your father was extremely proud of you. Your mother, too, of course. How is she, since—' His face flushed as he realised he'd walked right over the same minefield he'd only minutes before stumbled upon.

'She's well, thank you,' Nora hurried to answer, desperate to smooth the waters. 'She's actually visiting Jared in New York at the moment and helping him organise his wedding. And thank you for saying that about my father. It's very kind of you to say so,' she said as she bowed her head to accept the compliment with the question of whether her father really was proud of her ringing in her head.

She knew, in theory, he was, but sometimes, at the height of the anger, she wished with all her might for one last conversation. One last opportunity to tell him she loved him and ask him outright if he was proud of her. Proud of her as a person, not proud of her business acumen. Just once she would have liked to hear him tell her that. But their meeting ground had always been business, her fault she knew, because she had chosen the only language her father communicated in and made sure she mastered it.

Now even those moments of closeness were lost to her.

'Mr Love, it was nice to meet you,' Mr Collingsworth said. 'I'd better go and find my wife. Take her for that promised spin around the floor.'

When he'd disappeared from sight, Ethan turned to her with a gentle smile and said, 'Do you think that might be enough networking for this evening?'

Nora bent slightly at the waist to try and draw more air into her lungs. 'Oh, my God, I really made a mess of that.'

'Hey, you got caught unawares. That's all.'

She shook her head, unwilling to let herself off the hook, frustrated as always by her inability to behave perfectly in the face of the anger she couldn't seem to rid herself of. 'I totally embarrassed that man and made him feel awkward.'

'He recovered. So did you. Don't worry about it.'

Her throat ached in defeat. 'I owe you an apology, as well, for feeling as if you had to rush to my rescue when I know you were talking to some woman.'

Ethan stared speculatively at her for a long time and then smiled. 'I think to make up for it you'll almost certainly have to dance with me.'

Her laugh came without warning, shocking the last of the rage and discomfiture away. God, but he played havoc with that knot she tried to keep so secure inside herself. 'I suppose it's only fair,' she said, giving him a look of pure sufferance and eliciting one of his deep, throaty laughs that had her heart kicking out of her chest again. 'One dance and then I think it might be time to leave.'

'I'd better make it memorable, then,' he said, heat flashing in his eyes as he grasped her hand and turned to lead her out onto the dance floor.

Without breaking stride, he swiped the glass out of her hand and set it down with his on one of the tables.

Then, smoothly, he twirled her expertly around to face him. The look in his eyes dared her to allow herself to relax and enjoy what was about to happen, and as if her mind didn't need to be consulted, she took one step closer to him. He grinned outrageously, obviously under the impression that the impressiveness of him dragging her so purposefully onto the dance floor was written upon her face.

Was there anything this knight couldn't do, Nora wondered as his fingers splayed against the satin material of her dress, slowly pressing her into matching his movement to the sultry number the band was playing?

Heat flooded her, her heart beat crazily and a deep and throbbing awareness thrummed between them.

She had to tip her head way back to see into his blue eyes and the steady and silent, 'don't even think about going anywhere' command he communicated had her breath hitching and her hand clenching once against his chest before it moved to slide up and over his shoulder.

His hand tightened against the small of her back in response and he brought his head down to rest against the top of hers.

Nora released the breath she was holding as her body moulded itself to his, wrapping around him, subconsciously responding to the safety within his hold, but ready to tease for a more dangerous response as well.

The push-pull of desire took every spare piece of her focus, so that everything else simply melted away. Her eyes drifted shut. He was everything you could want to cling to when you needed comfort, when you needed soothing, when you needed healing.

An addiction in the making.

Her eyes sprang open.

She couldn't let herself slide into needing what he provided.

He was only in her life temporarily.

She had to be able to depend upon herself because being with Ethan might chase away all the second-guessing she was drowning in, but it wasn't going to keep her doubting every decision she made when she found herself once again out of his arms.

'Princess,' Ethan whispered in her ear, 'if you don't stop all that thinking and start enjoying the dancing I'm going to resort to dirtier means to get you to have some simple fun.'

Her head came up and with only half an idea of the temptation she was expressing in her wide eyes, demanded, 'Explain "dirtier means"?'

Ethan's eyes flashed and then hooded. 'How about I show you instead?'

She laid her head back down on his chest before she could say, 'how about you do' and swayed determinedly along to the music. 'See,' she said striving to keep her voice light, 'This is me not thinking. This is me enjoying the dancing.'

'Coward,' he said on a half-laugh, half-groan.

She was. Oh, but she didn't want to be. What she wanted was to heed Sephy's words and for once not pay credence to 'what ifs'. If she acted without thinking everything through first, could she trust Ethan to catch her afterwards? Could she trust herself?

Very aware that she had wandered off into thinking land again, she shifted against him and was suddenly saved from his velvet warning when the music stopped and the whistling feedback from a microphone scratched at her senses.

'Everyone, if I could have your attention?' Eleanor Moorfield asked as she climbed up onto a chair, microphone in hand.

Ethan stopped dancing and turned Nora around to stand in front of him, wrapped his arms around her waist and, once again, rested his chin on the top of her head.

'Thank you,' Eleanor said. 'As I've mentioned to most everyone, I have a little surprise for the last two hours of the evening. All of you know I'm moving my base from Italy back to London because I've wanted to settle back here in my home country for a long time. Italy has been very good to me and will always hold a warm place in my heart and I'm sure you've all heard about the earthquake in the region of Emilia-Romagna. Despite being based in Rome I have visited the area many times. I've watched the devastating news footage of communities wiped out at the epicentre of where the earthquake hit…'

Nora felt Ethan's arms tighten in a band of tension around her and, without thought, her hands enfolded his and squeezed comfortingly.

'…A casino is going to be set up where the dance floor is and I would dearly love it if you could spend some time at the tables playing and enjoying yourselves, with the only stipulation that all the money you win or lose goes to help provide aid to those displaced by the earthquake.'

A round of applause erupted from the room but Ethan didn't move until couples started leaving the dance floor area to make room for the gambling stations to be set up.

'We don't have to stay,' Nora told Ethan quietly, feeling cold as he unwound his arms from around her to shove his hands into his trouser pockets. 'We can make our excuses and leave right now.'

'I can handle it.'

Nora looked up at him. He had the sort of grim determination on his face usually reserved for things like trips to dentists.

'I'm really not sure you'll enjoy the gambling. Given the situation with Ryan—'

He shrugged his broad shoulders. 'I know. Ironic, right?'

He looked perfectly at ease. But she knew him better now and she knew those impressive shoulders of his had lifted a few millimetres.

'I'd be happy to leave a large donation before we leave,' she said, wanting to help him somehow.

The light absented itself from his eyes as his expression flattened out. 'And would that come from your own pocket, the Kings' pocket, or KPC's pocket?' he asked with a touch of bite.

Nora stared him down. 'I'd be happy for it to come from all three pockets, Ethan. This isn't about throwing money at a problem. Don't make it about your parents. A charity appeal doesn't care where the money comes from as long as it is legitimate and I'm pretty sure the families that need the money don't care either.'

As his blue eyes narrowed in warning, she refused to cower, wanting instead to make him understand that her privileged status had taught her the value of social responsibility along with the value of money. 'Look, I'm not trying to make you feel—'

His hand withdrew from his pocket to ward off her words. 'Fine. I get it. Like I said, I can handle it—unless you're saying you can't?'

The formality in his stance came as a shock after the fluid way he'd moved her about the dance floor, but she wasn't going to shy away from him, because hadn't he spent the majority of the evening looking out for her and helping her with an assuredness that didn't make her embarrassed or feel as if he was taking over, but rather, had her realising how immensely she respected him. 'No. Not at all. If you want to stay, then of course, I'm happy to.'

'Well, then,' he tipped his head and turned towards where the bar area was. 'I'll get us something stronger to drink and then let's go and make the appeal some money.'

Nora stood in the lift next to Ethan and entered the private code for the penthouse she lived in, anticipation almost tangible while she watched the numbers on the digital display flash by too quickly.

'I can't believe how much money you won on that last game of roulette,' she said and then felt her eyes go round because she was fairly convinced she'd already uttered the exact same words when they'd left the party and Ethan had insisted that the car take her back to her place first.

'I was lucky,' he said philosophically, but she suspected that there wasn't much Ethan wasn't good at.

'Are you wishing you were back there helping instead of here helping Ryan?'

'Yes.'

Another one-word answer but Nora found honour in his simple honesty. 'I know it's not the same, but in a small way tonight you at least got to continue that help.'

The lift stopped. She reached forward to press the button to open the lift doors, but her fingers paused.

She swallowed and said over her shoulder, 'Well. This is me,' and felt Ethan move to stand behind her.

His hand reached out to cover hers. 'Invite me in.'

His quiet command washed over her like silk.

She wanted to invite him in. Had been thinking about it all the way home in the car.

All the reasons not to seemed to have evaded her.

The entire evening, filled not just with flirting but with a loose friendship, now felt like a prelude—a long slow dance to this. To falling into each other.

Crazy.

If she did this and…her mind stumbled to a halt, somehow unwilling to take her thoughts beyond the red flag.

She turned her head and forced her gaze to meet his, needing to see what he was thinking.

'You know we're going to keep circling back to this,' he said persuasively. 'Invite me in.'

His blue eyes were serious.

His face a little flushed.

All while he waited patiently for her decision.

Dragging in a breath, she pressed the button to open the lift doors. Ethan's hand left hers and he stepped away to allow her space. Nora crossed the threshold into her home and turned around to face him. The lift doors signaled they were about to close and she reached out with a hand to keep them open.

Ethan didn't even hesitate before he stepped into her apartment, letting the doors swoosh shut behind him.

'Coffee?' she asked, her voice sounding high and as though it was coming from someone else.

Ethan shook his head, shoved his hands in his pockets and wandered over to the floor-to-ceiling windows to stare out at the London skyline.

'You have a lovely place,' he said as if he didn't really care.

'Thank you,' she answered as if she didn't really care, either.

Well this was…awkward.

Desperately needing something to do, Nora got her feet to move her over towards the kitchen area. She plonked her clutch on the plush L-shaped couch as she passed and when she reached the kitchen counter grabbed the kettle.

'Nora?' Ethan asked gently.

She paused with the kettle in her hand to find he had turned from the view to watch her.

'Do you want this?'

She breathed in deep. Honour in honesty. 'You know I do.'

'What's changed? Why have you stopped running away from it?'

'I don't exactly know,' she said, her heartbeat thundering in her ears.

'I won't let you pretend this hasn't happened afterwards.'

Her heart thundered harder. 'Okay.'

He seemed momentarily surprised. 'But this can only be temporary.'

'I know. I think I like it better this way.'

His lips lifted in a sexy smile. 'Then what are you doing all the way over there? Come here.'

Excitement skittered the length of her spine as she put down the kettle. Did she like receiving orders? She'd been the boss for so long, it was new—refreshing.

She walked slowly towards him, liking that his eyes got bluer. His jaw got tighter. His body got bigger.

Whether he felt bad about issuing such a command, or whether he couldn't wait for her to get to him, when he took two steps towards her, she loved that the attraction was mutual. Identical.

'Take off your coat,' he said, his voice deep as his eyes went to her belt buckle.

Her hands moved to the buckle and fumbled with the clasp. She tried a steadying breath. She could do this without the knot inside of her unravelling, couldn't she? Finally she got the material to give

119

and quickly she slid her fingers through the loops to separate the two ends. *Because maybe the knot was never meant to be undone.* She set about unbuttoning her coat and when she was finished, instead of parting the lapels and removing the jacket, she paused. What if the knot inside her came undone completely and…

Okay.

She needed not to think. 'Undo your bowtie and slip open the top button of your shirt,' she said back to him.

His smile was quick. 'Are we going to be vying for control the whole way through?'

'Won't it be fun to find out?' Fun. Simple. No space to think. She parted her coat and shrugged it off her shoulders and then watched as his hands went to his bowtie.

He really had such beautiful hands. Large. Strong. Capable. Dexterous. Exciting.

He flicked open the top button on his shirt and dropped his hand. She stared at the exposed skin and thought about how she was going to love putting her mouth there to taste him.

She must have licked her lips because he chuckled and lifting his hand, beckoned her with his fingers to close the last little distance between them.

The second she stepped into him, his arms shot out to wrap her against him and she was reminded once again of how tall he was, how broad his shoulders were and how sheltered she felt in his arms.

On tiptoes, she stretched up tall. Her hand reached up to tug aside the collar of his shirt and slowly she allowed the tip of her tongue to slide out and taste the gloriously golden skin where throat met shoulder.

Better than all the vanilla lattes in the world.

The blood turned heavy in her veins. Her eyes closed as she licked again and savoured the taste and the sensation of his throat working beneath her mouth as he swallowed. She wanted to bite. She wanted to suck.

As if he knew what she wanted because it was what he needed, he twisted his hand up into her hair to lock her in place and leaned back, exposing the tight cords so that she could run her mouth up the long column of his neck, nuzzle under and across his jawline to his earlobe and then close her mouth over his flesh and nip.

His breath came out on a short sharp groan and then his fingers were pulling against her scalp and he was wrenching her mouth away from his neck so that he could crush her mouth with his.

She fell hungrily into his kiss like she'd been waiting for it forever. His mouth moved over hers to ravish it with a rich and powerful intensity that claimed and then conquered like some Viking god.

She kissed him back with force; an equal warrior. His hands moved out of her hair and roamed over her body. Everywhere he touched her became soft and pliable as she caught on fire for him.

And now she couldn't breathe with the wanting of him.

If she could have done so, she'd have climbed right into him.

And the knowledge had that enduring knot loosening inside herself so that she thought she could feel it sliding dangerously free against her lungs.

Ethan plundered her mouth as his hands found the zip at the back of her dress and deftly tugged it open. Fingertips slid under the straps of her dress and eased it down, his hands splaying warmly against her waist as he slid the material over her hips so that the heavy satin material rustled to the floor, leaving her in matching silk underwear and her new heels. When she felt the cool air flash across her skin before she felt the sinfully hot goodness of his palms shaping her buttocks, her breath came quickly. Much too quickly.

Scarily quick.

'Wait.' She tore her mouth away to drag in air as she pushed against his chest. He loosened his hold instantly but kept his hands on her.

'Wait? Okay. I can do that. I think,' he said, smiling as he too breathed hard. 'I thought you enjoyed fast?'

'I do,' she heaved air into her lungs. 'I just need to get my breath back.'

She felt a gentle caress against her back. 'We'll slow things down,' he told her, trailing his fingertip across her collarbone and she saw his expression turn thoughtful and intense as he added, 'Although I might need you to be a little less…responsive. It's really hot when you tremble for me like that.'

Her eyes closed and her breath hitched. On second thoughts, if he slowed things down too much, he'd have her losing her breath completely.

'Maybe we should make the pace up as we go along?' she managed to say. A little fast, a little slow, a lot fast again. Might give her a shooting chance of maintaining some sort of breathing pattern to survive the experience.

His gaze moved from where his fingertips were slowly stroking to look deep into her eyes. The skin at the corner of his lashes crinkled in understanding and the next thing she knew he was bending at the knees and sweeping her up into his arms, as if she weighed nothing, and making off down the corridor with her.

Viking warrior all over again.

She giggled.

Giggled.

In her bedroom he lowered her slowly to her feet and all trace of giggling left her as she stood in front of him, suddenly nervous again because now he was looking at her as she stood in front of him in the bright light of her bedroom, in her underwear and shoes, with her hair a mess and goodness knows what emotions shining in her eyes.

Ethan reached out and pulled the clips from her hair, smoothing the black silky strands back behind her ears in a gesture she found both sweet and sexy. His thumb skated over her jawline and tenderly tipped up her chin as he lowered his mouth to hers.

This time his kisses were slower, a drugging pleasure, as if he were the ultimate adventurer and had all the time in the world to explore. Her hands came out to lock onto his forearms and when she couldn't speed him up she moved them up to his chest so that her fingers could occupy themselves unbuttoning his shirt. When she fumbled with the last button, he helped her, making quick work of releasing the white cotton from his tux trousers.

As soon as her hands touched the bare skin of his chest, she broke the kiss in order to feast with her eyes.

In appreciation of what she saw, she trailed her fingers down his pecs, over his nipples and down, down, luxuriating in the undulating hard ridges of his abs.

Beneath her touch Ethan went stock-still so she brought her hands all the way back up, retracing every delicious inch to slip them under the material of his shirt and push it off his chest. The shirt slipped down his arms and still he didn't move. She removed his cufflinks slowly. Concentrating fully. Not noticing he kicked off his shoes. When the shirt dropped to the floor, she took a step back to admire. She didn't think she'd ever had such a toned and honed torso to play with.

He was the absolute best marketing tool for his business Love Leisure. Anyone getting a look at this would be signing up for exclusive membership in a split second.

Her eyes moved to the tattoo that wrapped around his chest, and following the dragon's tail she stepped to the side and around to take in his magnificent back. Her hands reached up to lay upon his shoulders and when her thumbs stroked up and over the top of his spine, his head dropped forward on a deep sigh. All that musculature under her fingertips felt incredibly powerful. Looking her fill as the ripple effect of her touch moved down his spine, she found what she had been seeking. As her hands slipped from his shoulders to glide slowly down his arms, she gently leaned forward, locked her fingers around his hands and held on as she kissed the dragon's tail at the centre of his back.

She felt the shudder rip through him and smiled against his back, 'I like it when you tremble for me too.'

Chapter Nine

Ethan turned in one fluid motion, picked her up, wrapped her legs around his hips and took her mouth again and again and again.

Faster now.

Hungrier now.

The silk comforter was a cool shock against her skin as he lowered her onto the bed, but the chill lasted only a second before he followed her down, surrounding her once again with his size and heat.

She moaned as his lips grazed the column of her neck. Her hands flew to his back to cling as his fingers dragged the cup of her bra away from her breast and when he took her nipple into his mouth her hips arched off the bed in need.

'I think I'm going to need you to go even faster, after all,' she groaned out.

He chuckled against her, raising a thousand goose bumps that chased each other over her skin. 'Oh, you're not nearly needy enough for fast, yet.'

'I'm not?' She could feel how wet she already was for him.

He unhooked the front clasp of her bra and turned his attention to her other breast and whispered confidently, 'Nope. Not yet,' before taking her into his mouth.

Nora released another moan as her sucked her nipple into the wet cavern of his mouth, igniting a white-hot flame that had her squeezing her eyes tight shut.

He took his time moving down her body, his large hands shaping her thighs, running down the length of her calves and brushing over her shoes.

Her shoes.

Lord, she still had her shoes on.

Ethan moved to kneel between her legs, holding her right foot he extended her leg to his chest level, his hands moving caressingly across the straps of her shoe as he unbuckled the strap. Gently removing her shoe, he grinned and then tossed it theatrically over her shoulder.

'Hey, careful, those are brand-new,' she pouted.

Ethan merely lifted his eyebrow in reply and gestured for her to lift her other foot, no doubt so that it could receive the same treatment. She thought about it for precisely one second before concluding she could always buy more new shoes.

She raised her left leg and placed her foot in his hands. He paid slow and thorough attention to the straps again before removing it to toss it artlessly over his shoulder to join the other one.

His thumbs pressed hard into the arch of her foot and her breath released on a whimper as her hips arched off the bed towards him. He seemed to like the movement of her body as it sought more contact with his because his thumbs pressed again to see if she repeated the action.

Wanting to pay him back a little for his easy manipulation of her body, she trailed her free foot down his magnificent chest to settle in his crotch.

She pressed the sole of her foot against his erection and smiled a thoroughly wicked smile. He grinned back and, covering her foot with his hand, moved against her a few times, before bringing her leg up again to rest at his shoulder.

Sliding his hands down the length of her legs, he reached the lace trim of her underwear, hooked his thumbs under the elastic, drew them off and threw them over his shoulder to land near her shoes.

She trembled as he pressed a kiss to the underside of her knee. Bit her lip and moved against him when his mouth slid a couple of inches further down to taste her thigh.

'You have really fantastic long legs, Nora.'

In answer she undulated impatiently, eager for him to reach his ultimate destination.

His laugh broke free against the top of her thigh and then her eyes were crossing in pleasure as he sealed his mouth against her core.

Her hands clutched against the silk comforter as Ethan's wicked tongue did delicious things to her.

Surely now he could taste how much she needed him. How she was completely at his mercy.

Whether she begged aloud she would never know because as his tongue flicked over her clitoris, her body flexed and she flew into a million pieces.

She was still trembling from the first rush of orgasm as he kissed and licked his way back up her body. Moved his mouth to her ear and whispered, 'I'm thinking now we go a little faster.'

'Okay,' she answered, willing to grant him anything. 'Oh. Condoms,' she realised and turned to clamber back up the bed to her nightstand. She opened the drawer and removed a box, hands shaking, not with nerves but with anticipation of the more to come, as she broke open the box and trickled a few out onto the bed.

Laughter bubbled out of her when Ethan grabbed her playfully by the ankle and tugged, turning her around and having her lying back on the bed easily. In the time it had taken her to get to the condoms, he'd removed the rest of his clothes.

She passed a foil packet to him and watched through half-shut eyes as he ripped it open and sheathed himself.

When he settled himself over her she was once again surrounded by his scent, his feel, his strength and it occurred to her that she was exactly where she'd been wanting to be and that it felt as wonderful as she'd imagined. More so, even. She moaned as he entered her in one powerful, smooth thrust. Her hands locked onto his in fear she was going to fly right out of herself far too quickly. But he simply smiled gently down at her and started moving.

'Keep your eyes open for me,' he insisted.

'I can't...oh,' she moved under him, already eagerly chasing the pleasure.

'You can. I need to see you.'

How could he possibly doubt she was with him one hundred percent when her body was flowing under him, straining under him, needing what only he seemed qualified to give.

'I'm here. I'm in this with you,' she promised.

At her words he moved harder, faster and she matched him thrust for thrust, surrendering her emotions inch by inch and laying her soul bare to him because she couldn't not with him. He made it too powerful, too beautiful, too...everything.

The higher her soul soared the more she realised it was because she was tethered so safely to him.

Her fingers tightened against his, her thighs gripped harder and her body bowed up into his as she started to climax. 'Ethan,' she called out his name as she started to spiral up and up, faster and higher than she ever had before, 'Don't let me fall too hard,' she whispered.

'Never,' he answered, stroking up into her once, twice and then throwing back his head to growl out his own release.

Ethan stared down at Nora with what he suspected was a sort of smitten geeky smile on his face.

She was sleeping.

She still had a satisfying rose bloom on her skin and he loved that he'd been the one to put it there.

God, she'd been so responsive.

So alive.

So participative.

He hadn't expected, hadn't prepared himself for such an uninhibited response during their first time together.

When it came to sex, Nora King didn't hold back emotionally. Or was it him that had pulled that special response from her?

He breathed deeply, taking her scent along with the oxygen down to the bottom of his lungs.

Was it that important that he be the one to wring such unrestrained pleasure from her?

Yes.

He could be honest enough to admit that. The fact that she pulled such a response from him. Of course he wanted it to be equal.

When he had to leave, it would be easier on them both if everything was felt equally and dealt with equally. He needed them to remain friendly.

He steeled himself against the instinctive reaction that, after what they'd shared, it was going to be hard to leave.

But he had commitments. He'd made a promise.

And he'd been very careful not to make Nora a promise he'd have to break.

He counted the tiny freckles across the bridge of her nose that appeared now that the sheen of light makeup had worn off and resisted leaning down to kiss them in case he woke her.

She moved in her sleep.

Closer to him, and giving into the need building inside him, he trailed his fingers slowly down her arm.

Her skin was so smooth and milky-white. She looked fragile. Ethereal. Kind of like how he imagined a real wood nymph to be, rather than the models dressed up at the party.

The many sides of Nora King had him quite fascinated.

She didn't seem to know it, but she was anything but fragile and in no way was she brittle, either.

Why she was so afraid of letting go, when the results as she did so were breathtaking, confused him, saddened him and at the same time made him feel that he'd been privy to something rare; as if he knew a secret about her now that she didn't share with the rest of the world.

Without warning she opened her eyes and focused straight in on him, an intelligent frown instantly forming as she drank him in with her eyes.

'You haven't slept at all?' She reached up to lay her hand against his cheek, her concern bewitching.

'I'm okay,' he answered and tried to ignore that he couldn't remember the last time someone would have been worried to discover he wasn't sleeping.

Her smile was soft. 'Only okay?' She pouted a little. 'Hmmn. I guess still being awake is better than falling asleep in the middle. Although, how you can still be awake after that..?' she crossed her eyes.

He chuckled. 'I've enjoyed watching you sleep.' Something vulnerable peaked through her eyes and he wanted to dispel it immediately. 'In an entirely non-creepy way,' he joked.

'Was I sleeping, or was I out cold? I think you short-circuited something somewhere.'

They smiled at each other.

'Hey. I have an idea,' she said, rising up, uncaring about the sheet slipping from her breasts.

'Does it involve me checking your circuits?' he said, his gaze lowering to her breasts.

'More the other way around. I give a really good massage. I must have some oils somewhere.' She sprang out of bed, full of energy.

He wasn't used to someone wanting to make sure he was all right; he was used to it being the other way around. What if he liked it too much? What if that made it harder to leave when the time came? 'Nora, it's really kind of you to be worried about me not sleeping, but I'm okay.'

'Well then enjoy the massage anyway.' She sauntered over to

the doorway and turned the dimmer switch down to bathe the room in a much softer light. 'Face down on the bed, please. I'll be back in a second.'

Ethan stared up at the light prisms the chandelier threw out all over her ceiling and smiled. That she ordered him about with such a light touch was kind of sweet. Nora might have been felled by her grief recently, but she was on the way back from it and he had a feeling the world had better watch out when she arrived. He breathed in—maybe he'd better watch out too. She was already halfway under his skin. All the way under and he'd have himself a whole lot of trouble.

He breathed out.

Sleep would be good. Give him that break from thinking. Maybe the massage would ease the way.

He turned over and got himself settled on the bed, resting his head on his forearms. If she wanted to give him a massage, who was he to complain?

'Close your eyes,' she commanded softly as she padded back into the room.

'But I was enjoying the view,' he said, taking in her sexy nakedness.

'How about if I promise that the view will still be here after?'

Ethan frowned as the knowledge that she shouldn't be making him promises when he couldn't make any back, sat uncomfortably inside him.

'Ethan, close your eyes for me,' she said again, her tone firm.

His heart thumped heavily as he did as he was bid because he'd asked her to keep her eyes *open* for him and she had. She'd kept them open and let him in, in a beautiful display of courage and trust. Not one ounce of judgement present. God, he really hoped he didn't mess up and abuse the faith she'd placed in him by opening herself up to him like she had.

He felt the bed dip slightly as she got on and knelt beside him.

'I couldn't find my oils so I'm using some moisturiser. Relax, it'll shower off in the morning,' she said, misunderstanding the tightening in his shoulders when her hands made first contact with his skin. 'You won't be leaving here smelling all girly.'

As her hands travelled the length of his back, he thought he might have discovered another state of bliss.

And all he could smell was her.

All he could feel was her.

All he wanted was her.

Again and again and again.

Like an addiction.

He frowned into his arms and turned his head the other way from her.

'Where did you get your dragon done?' she asked after a few minutes.

'Here and there,' he mumbled into his arm, sighing as she stroked and kneaded.

'Huh?'

'I got the head done in Scotland, the body in Mexico, the tail,' he frowned harder, 'on the way back from Syria.'

'But why not get it done in one sitting, in one place?'

Ethan's brain worked overtime worrying about how weird he would sound if he leant words to the actual reason, but whether it was because magic was flowing out of her hands or because she'd asked so simply, he surprised himself when the words started flowing. 'It's, I don't know—it's a sort of ritual thing I do now. The first time I went to Scotland to help with a landslide after snowmelt, I met up with a few of the locals the night before we left, got very drunk and woke up the next day with half a tattoo. I've got no idea at all why it was only half- finished. The following year I got invited back for one of the guys' weddings. It was summer rather than winter so everything looked different—different good. Different better. Whether it was in that spirit, or, most probably because I was drunk again on the stag night, I decided to have a bit more of the tattoo done. And so now, whenever I get to re-visit a place I've worked in I add a bit more of the tattoo.'

'Oh.'

The word came out on a sort of enlightened-sounding sigh and he couldn't help it, he tensed up again and she must have been able to feel it under her hands. When the seconds ticked by and she didn't say anything more, he felt it necessary to add, 'It's just a dumb form of closure—don't go thinking it's romantic or something.'

'Actually I think it's quite logical. When you go back you're seeing the area differently to how it was the last time you were there. Why not celebrate that? I think it's lovely and fitting. It's like you're imprinting a different image of the place to replace your last one.'

'I won't always be able to get back to particular locations.'

'So you'll get the dragon completed in different places and think of the help you provided and that you had an effect on the situation and the people there.'

Damn, he liked her.

She got it.

She totally got it.

'You only have a little colour left to do in the tail anyway. Perhaps you'll get it done when you go back to Italy.'

He grunted, because despite her soothing strokes he could feel the tightness returning to coil deep inside him.

'Was the earthquake very bad?'

'I wasn't in it. We always arrive after.' Had that sounded dismissive? Her hands pressed along either side of his spine and he inhaled as deeply as he could and let the breath out slowly to match her rhythm.

'Then why can't you sleep?'

'I don't know.' He concentrated with all his might on the feel of his muscles being lengthened under her hands.

'I think you do.'

He tried concentrating harder. 'I really don't. If I did, I'd be

132

sleeping, wouldn't I?'

'It might help to tell me,' she said, her voice as soothing as her hands.

He sighed. 'It won't change anything.'

'How do you know?' Her hands left his back and he felt strangely marooned, but in the next instant he heard her opening the bottle of moisturiser again.

The minute her hands returned to his back, he said, 'I went into a building to help get a little boy out.' He frowned against his forearms. He hadn't expected to allow the words to tumble out but her coaxing was like her ordering him about, deft and light.

She didn't say anything. Not one single thing. Her hands merely carried on their sweet stroking. Up and down and sometimes spanning out to sweep over his shoulders.

On their next sweep of his shoulders, he continued, 'There was an aftershock while we were in there and some of the building came down on us, making it difficult to get out.'

Up and down. Up and down, her touch eased. Soothed.

'There wasn't anyone to help and so it took some time,' he added, squeezing his eyes shut in the crook of his arm as in his head he went straight back to that place.

'But you got him out unhurt?'

'Yes. He was fine—a few cuts and bruises.'

'And other than the cut to your hand, you were fine?'

So she *had* noticed that. 'Yes. Fine. No damage done at all.'

Except the damage he'd created to his reputation by going into that building alone and without telling anyone.

'That little boy was very lucky to have you there, Ethan. Very lucky.'

He grunted again.

'It must have been so scary,' she whispered, the graveness in her voice pulling at him.

'He was a trooper.'

'I meant for you. The responsibility you had to shoulder—being

133

the adult who had to remain calm. You must have analysed the situation you were in and understood the ramifications of the aftershock...'

Her hands never once broke their rhythm and he wanted to congratulate her on her courage, trying to help tame the dragon inside him like she was. His heart thudded dangerously as he came closer to admitting to her than he had even to himself how scared he'd been. What he'd realised in that dark and dusty cave of rubble.

'Was it noisy?'

'What?'

'Was it noisy in that building with the little boy?'

'Not really. The noises were deep, you know? Like quiet rumbles and creaks every now and then. Sporadic.' *Plenty of time to think.* 'Mostly all I could feel was the ground shaking under us.'

'You said at the party that you'd seen conflict. You mentioned Syria, so I'm guessing you were part of a team providing aid during the conflict there?'

The sudden change in direction had his guard coming up and his breathing coming quicker until her hands once again worked their magic. 'I went over with a consignment of tents, water filters, water carriers, insect nets, etc. Logistically it's tricky. You have to be able to distribute any aid you bring over discreetly so that your group doesn't become a target for looters and suchlike.'

He waited for her to ask if they'd become a target. Waited to tell her that nothing bad had happened at all. That it was what it was. They went. They distributed the aid. They came back. No big deal.

'Must've been noisy sometimes,' she said instead. 'Not all the time, but when you didn't expect it, you know? And the ground must have shaken with the force of—'

The bed shook as he turned over, lightning-quick, to face her.

'Don't,' he barked out as the shame in him broke free. 'Don't you dare try and psychoanalyse me. You think I can't sleep because what happened in that building reminded me of being in Syria?' His heart was beating a crazy scary tattoo against his chest wall.

134

'You think it's that easy? You think it's that simple? You think now you've established a connection that I'll be able to sleep? You think a couple of conversations and some sex and suddenly you *know* me? Suddenly you can fix me? And you accused me of trying to save you. Well, Princess, let me tell you that —Jesus, you're crying.' The shock shut the dragon inside of him right up. 'Hey, don't cry. Why are you crying? I shouldn't have shouted like that. I've scared you.'

Nora shook her head at him. 'You think I'm afraid of a little shouting?'

Then why was she crying? For him? His hand shook as he reached out to brush away a tear. 'You have to stop.' Guilt tinged with panic. He didn't want her judgement. 'Don't feel sorry for me.'

'I don't feel sorry for you, you idiot,' she rebuked, palming away more tears as they spilled over. 'I feel proud to know you.'

Ethan recoiled. 'You don't know what you're saying.' If she knew that he'd been sent home from the earthquake site because he'd broken protocol she wouldn't feel so proud to know him, would she?

'I do, actually. I'm saying that your compassion for people… the work you do, moves me. I'm saying I appreciate your ability to tolerate difficult conditions in order to help people you've never even met.'

'No.' He shook his head in denial. 'You're making it sound something it's not.'

Her smile was watery and extra-patient as she looked at him. 'Ethan, for your job, do you go into stressful situations and help people so that they can survive to help themselves?'

'Yes. But anyone with the specific training I've had can do that.'

'But do they *want* to? That's the real question, isn't it?'

'I—'

'Your work requires you to want to be in uncertain, dangerous, unstable places, when you could be somewhere familiar, easy and safe. I imagine you will have seen humanity at its worst, but also

135

people at their best. Don't say your passion for what you do doesn't mean anything. Your passion is part of what moves me.'

'You have passion for what you do.'

She blinked. 'Mine's a more selfish passion.'

'How do you know I don't do what I do purely for selfish reasons—egotistical reasons?'

'I don't think you do. But even if you did, you still help people, right?' She leant in and placed the gentlest of kisses at the base of his throat. 'Right?' she asked again, moving to place a kiss at the corner of his mouth.

'Yes,' he admitted before taking her mouth with his so that he could take them both under. Swap one intimacy for another. One he had more control over. One she made him want, simply by looking at him. By telling him he moved her...

She broke the kiss to drag in air and he could see a steely, determined look in her eyes and he knew he should be wary, but how could he be when she was so endearing, so intelligent, so sexy and now looking at him so seductively?

'You're so busy helping others. Who helps you, Ethan?' The words were peppered with butterfly kisses to his chest as she pushed him backwards to lie on the bed.

He groaned as her fingernails scraped like a temptress down his sides and as he went rock-hard beneath her he fought to remember the question.

'Who helps you, Ethan?' she repeated as she moved lithely over his body. He wanted to tell her he didn't need help. That he was perfectly fine. But as he lifted his head to look down at her and opened his mouth to tell her so, he caught the light in her eyes. Remembered the way she had kept her eyes open for him and instead found himself reaching for her to bring her into alignment with his body and bury his head in her neck so that he could whisper, 'You have. You've helped me.'

At his admission, she leaned back to stare into his eyes. Whatever she saw there had her smile turning proud and confident. She sat up on him and reached for one of the foil packets left on the bed from earlier. She tore it open with her teeth and put it on him.

Her laugh was pure seduction when he groaned as she sat back on him.

'You going to ride me like you ride that motorbike of yours?' he gasped out as she took him in her hand and rose above him.

'Better hold on tight,' she teased as she sank down onto him taking him all the way deep inside herself.

His hands flexed at her waist. She had no idea what it did to him to see her rising above him, her hands at her breasts, her eyes dilated, her mouth dropping open in pleasure. The warrior princess celebrating victory in battle, the battle he'd been waging against himself, the battle to try and heal himself.

He could feel himself letting go with every stroke. Feel himself getting closer with every pretty circle of her hips.

But he needed to be closer. As close as he could get. Needed her eyes to be open for him again. Needed to know absolutely that it wasn't only the mindless pleasure of great sex but something more that turned her eyes to shimmering jet—something intrinsic to the two of them and what she'd made him share with her.

He moved into a sitting position, loving the surprise flashing through her eyes.

'I see you. I'm right here. My eyes are open,' she promised.

He tried desperately not to hurt her as his hands on her hips tightened to urge her on faster, stronger, deeper, until he thought his heart was going to burst free of his chest.

Her hands drove into his hair and gripped hard onto his scalp as he buried his head in her neck.

'Ethan...it's too much, I can't hold on. I'm going to come all over you,' she gasped out.

The roaring in his ears deafened him and he threw back his head, held her down onto him hard and shouted, 'Do it,' as they came together.

Chapter Ten

'And he sleeps,' Nora whispered to herself with a satisfied smile on her face.

Carefully she pushed back the sheet and got up from the bed.

She could have stayed like she was for the remainder of the night, tucked into his side, watching over him while he slept. But he needed his rest and she didn't want him to sense her watching. She wanted him to sleep the sleep he deserved.

She took her robe off the hook on the back of the bedroom door and slipped into it. Padding out to the lounge area she made a detour to the kitchen breakfast bar and poured herself a glass of wine from the open bottle on the side. Her lips were already curving into another smile as she brought the glass to her lips to take her first sip.

So.

Wow.

She felt all soft and mellow for the first time in she didn't know how long.

She felt satisfied.

Like *completely* satisfied.

Apparently that's what happened when you had mind-blowing, world-altering sex with a six-foot-six giant who took the lead and gave it back to you so you could share everything in between.

There was no room for guilt when you'd gloried in such care and attention.

No room for regret.

There was simply joy.

She brought the wineglass to her lips again, took another sip and then walked over to stand in front of the windows.

Staring out at the London skyline, she let go of all the times recently where she'd felt lonely staring at the same view. She couldn't afford to compare the before with the now because this thing with Ethan was only temporary and she needed to let herself enjoy it for what it was.

Two people coming together to heal from very different things.

Idly she wondered if that was what it had felt like for him too.

She'd like it better if it was.

But if all it was, was the sex for him—then that was fine too.

Something he could enjoy and keep as a memory before he had to revisit the dark memories he'd brought with him from Italy.

She wandered over to her writing desk in the far corner of the room and pulled out the Queen Anne-style chair. She turned it a little to face the window—one of her favourite places to sit. Close enough to the window to see the illuminated buildings, but far enough away so that she could sit in shadow and think.

As she set down her wineglass on the cluttered surface beside her, her gaze snagged on the middle drawer of her desk and before she knew what she was giving herself permission to do, she opened the drawer and stared at the letter inside.

A split-second hesitation and then she was reaching in and withdrawing the heavy envelope. Holding it with the pads of her forefingers pressed to opposite corners, she felt the comforting crisp linen blend of paper press into her. Spinning the letter between her fingertips, she stared at it. The internal debate about when or whether she should open it never stopped.

With a sigh, she dropped the letter to her lap, held one hand over it in a protective reflex, and resumed staring out the window.

She felt so at peace she thought she might be able to hear her father's last words to her and accept them into her heart.

But would his words add to the wonderful feeling or would they wipe out all the healing she'd found in Ethan's arms?

She was scared of finding out and scared of never having the courage to find out.

She'd been working so hard for so long at KPC. Sometimes it felt as though all she was doing was running to stand still. Had all the responsibility, the worry, the sheer hard slog, worn away her love for it all? Surely it couldn't solely be grief that had led her to this emptiness, could it?

She searched for answers in the night sky beyond the window. She wished she was like Sephy and had opened her letter and read it as soon as she had got it. She wished she had x-ray vision so she could tell if the words inside would wipe out all the horrible second-guessing as to why her father had found it so easy to gift her KPC when he had retired. Had it really been because he had trusted in her abilities? That's what she wanted it to say. That's what she *needed* it to say. Not that it had simply been because she'd been the only King who'd wanted it.

She swallowed down some of the ruby-red wine as the admission that had been tangled up within that huge knot inside her slid into her consciousness in a way she finally understood.

How could she have truly proved her worth to run KPC when all she had done her whole time running the company was follow her father's carefully laid-out examples?

She didn't feel like a leader. She felt like a follower, only the mentor she had been following was no longer around to support and advise.

That was the truth she was afraid of reading in black and white.

That was the truth she was afraid she'd infer even if the words weren't actually there.

Her father had never been one to flatter or praise and she'd learned not to expect those things from him. Learned not to need them in order to succeed. But in mourning for him she'd realised not pressing for either of those things hadn't added to her confidence but gradually taken away from it.

She was left worrying that she was a good lieutenant but a poor commander.

She should have tested herself and pressed for his praise so that she would have known unequivocally, one way or another, that he genuinely had faith in her ability to run the company on her own. But she'd felt she'd already impinged on her relationship with him by asking question after question about Jared when he'd left. All those months spent forcing the issue and her father never once responding...

She'd learned, hadn't she, that forcing the issue didn't win the prize?

Quickly she put the letter back where it now lived and slid the drawer quietly and tightly shut.

She didn't want to read something that might not give her the answers she needed and she didn't want her insides reforming into familiar knots that Ethan had so expertly undone.

She wanted to be happy.

And crawling back into her bed and tucking herself up beside Ethan was going to achieve that.

If only temporarily.

'What time is it?' Ethan asked as he stood in the doorway, squinting at the grey morning light pooling in through Nora's lounge windows.

'A little after ten,' she answered, looking up from where she was sat cross-legged on her huge sofa. Her laptop was perched precariously on top of her knees and papers seemed to take up every other available surface.

'I slept,' he declared, rubbing his hand over the back of his head and unsuccessfully smothering another yawn.

'You did,' she agreed.

He felt…better, lighter and God, she looked pretty, he thought, with her hair shoved into a neat ponytail high on her head, not a trace of makeup and that huge grin lighting up her face. All pleased-as-punch with herself, with very good reason.

Last night she'd taken care of him exquisitely.

He didn't know whether it was how she'd got him to unburden himself coupled with the massage and sex, but it had all resulted in a magnificent demonstration that she had faith in him.

She leaned over to pick up her coffee mug, grimacing when it was obviously empty. 'I bet you could do with a coffee too, huh?' she asked getting up from the sofa.

Ethan nodded and as she passed by him on her way to the glossy white kitchen area he caught hold of her free hand to halt her. Frowning down at her hand, so small in his, he was suddenly unsure how to say thank you without sounding as if what she had done for him last night was in any way easy, or something anyone would have taken the time to do. 'Nora—'

She reached up to lay her fingertips against his lips. 'No thanks necessary. Think of it as an eye-opener for me, at least now I know that if KPC ever goes belly-up—'

'You could have a very successful career as a psychoanalyst,' he finished for her.

'I was thinking masseuse or sleep-whisperer or something,' she finished shyly, dropping her hand away.

'Don't do that.'

'What?'

'I don't normally talk about that stuff with anyone, so don't belittle what you did.'

'I'm not,' she insisted, pride stiffening her shoulders.

'All right not belittle, then, but I've noticed you take your achievements and brush them aside as if they are nothing incredible, as though they don't deserve praise or an acknowledgement or a thank you.'

'Bad habit, I guess,' Nora turned abruptly, effectively ending the

142

conversation as she reached into an overhead cupboard to retrieve another mug. Pouring hot coffee from a jug, she indicated a bowl of sugar on the counter and opened the fridge to take out milk.

Ethan watched her movements in silence and tried to navigate the 'morning after' to make it easier on both of them because, truth to tell, after last night, he wanted as many morning afters with her as he could get.

Finally she wiped her hands nervously down her thighs and, looking up at him, asked, 'So, um, did you have plans for today?'

He had planned to drive down to visit Ryan and then had been going to spend some time on the phone seeing if he could find out if Pietro's family was accounted for, but selfishly, when he saw the shyness in her eyes, all he wanted to do was drag her back to bed, where she had been anything but shy with him, and keep her there until she knew she didn't have to be shy with him at any time. Anywhere. Ever. So instead he said with a warm smile, 'I don't have anywhere I'm expected.'

'Excellent. How would you like to drive down to Heathstead with me and take a look at a couple of properties that might be suitable for Love Leisure?'

'Wow. Okay. That so wasn't where I thought this was going.'

Nora managed to look innocent and not-understanding even as she grinned and continued, 'I was thinking that afterwards maybe we could have lunch with Sephy and update her.'

'On?' He teased.

'On your progress for Ryan. Not us. Obviously.'

She looked all shy again and he had to remind himself to go gently. 'Sounds like a plan. I'll need to stop by the hotel to pick up some fresh clothes—'

'Okay. You can shower here first, if you want,' she asserted, her smile growing slowly from shy to seductive, as if she felt on surer ground.

Ethan's own smile grew as he walked slowly towards her. 'You've probably got one of those state-of-the-art multi-jet showers, right?

Want to help me figure out the perfect combination of water and heat?'

'Oh, I'm sure I could find the time to give you instruction,' she quipped, all trace of her previous bashfulness banished now as her eyes ran over his naked chest as she picked up her coffee and drank thirstily.

Ethan jerked his thumb towards the sofa. 'But what about your work; it looks as if you were right in the thick of things.'

'I only have a little more reading to do. I can finish that off while you're back at your hotel picking up fresh clothes.' She stared at him over the rim of her coffee mug. 'You know, it's a shame tuxes aren't required uniform for Saturdays. If they were, you could have a workout downstairs in one of your very own branches of Love Leisure while I finished up here and then we could head out.'

'Of course,' Ethan said as something clicked into place. 'I wondered why the name of your building sounded so familiar.' He reached out to pull her into his arms. 'So you've been using my equipment for some time, then?'

'I have.' She pressed herself against him and ran her hands down and around to grip his butt-cheeks and give a playful squeeze. 'And on the subject of workouts, your personal equipment compares quite favourably.'

'Only quite?'

She shrieked out a laugh as he picked her up and headed down the corridor to her bathroom. 'Princess, you are about to be shown the maximum-intensity workout. Think you can handle it?'

'Well I'll certainly give it my all,' she assured as she sealed her lips to his.

Ethan wandered around the empty building thinking about all the work that would have to be done to make it into one of the Love Leisure high-end gyms. For this particular building to represent Love Leisure it would have to be completely gutted. He couldn't see it ever housing state-of-the-art equipment or the newest workout

144

trends within the time frame he had available to him.

The sharp stiletto clicks of Nora's boots drew his attention as she marched into the interior, making notes on her tablet as she went.

He wondered if she had any idea that the tip of her tongue poked out when she was concentrating.

She was ridiculously sexy in work mode.

His lips tipped up at the corners. Who was he kidding?—she was sexy in *breathing* mode.

And so damn likeable, it was scary.

He liked the way she was so fiercely protective of Sephy.

Liked the way she'd suited up and gone out and found Jared to help her keep KPC safe and running.

And *loved* the way she had been with him last night.

She definitely wasn't only the one-track-business-minded professional that he usually steered clear of.

She was intelligent, resilient, quirky, strong, and had a sense of humour.

God, she'd be good out in the field, leading her own team of rapid-response workers. Or logistics—making sure aid got to where it was needed speedily, efficiently and safely.

Whoa.

Ethan whipped his head back to stare at the wall and try to bring his thoughts under control. This was not one of those 'let's convert everyone to my passion', thing. This was sex…and something else…like friendship.

The question was; was it the type of real friendship that could conceivably weather drinks or dinner out whenever he was back in London.

'Can I be perfectly honest?' Nora asked, interrupting his thoughts.

He braced his feet apart, preparing for her to argue the friend-ship part, *preparing to argue back*, then realised she was looking around the room, not looking to argue what he had been thinking.

'Of course,' he replied feeling like an idiot and not liking the sudden spike in his heart-rate.

'This property isn't going to work for you. Not unless—'

'We knock through into the adjacent shop unit to double the space,' he finished for her, determined to get his head in the same work space as she so easily had.

She smiled and nodded. 'Shall we move onto the next property then, it's only a couple of streets away.'

'Sure. Let's go.'

He held the door open for her and caught the scent she'd been wearing last night. He wished he knew what it was. He could see himself, the next time he was at the airport waiting to board his plane, going through all the perfumes on sale trying to find the one that would remind him of her.

They walked side by side down Heathstead's peaceful tree-lined high street. It was hard to believe they were only about twenty miles from London. When his parents had been living here with Ryan, he'd been finishing up university and had never taken the time to visit during holidays. Holidays were for working at the charity and making trips out to Africa to help build schools. All of that was still less hard work than being at home would have been.

The vibe here was relaxed and pleasant; giving him a boost to think that Ryan was going to have a real shot at making a new start here. 'It must be nice living in one place for the majority of your life,' he said.

'I guess you've never really had that,' Nora mused. 'Have you got a place somewhere that you always come back to?'

'I have a base, but a permanent address seems like hassle when I'm away so much.' Ethan suddenly realised how that might look; the fact that he usually stayed in a luxury hotel that housed one of the biggest Love Leisure gyms near to his headquarters in Hull whenever he was back for a while.

He'd always intended to buy a property and turn it into a home, something he could rely on remaining the same, no matter which corner of the world he was living in. But somehow he'd never got around to it. The more time had passed the more he'd assumed that he was too used to living in temporary accommodation to know how to live in one place. Most times he came back he got restless within a few weeks.

'I suppose there's no real point letting a place stay empty for most of the year,' Nora agreed, surprising him. 'For me, I'll always think of this place as where I came from. I went away to school and university and I've been living in London for three years now, which I love, but maybe I love it so much because I know this is where the family homestead is. At least I hope it always will be.'

The tremble in her voice was barely noticeable but he was so attuned to her he heard it. 'There's a chance your mother might sell up now?'

'Mmn.' She shot him a quick smile and shrugged her shoulders, as if to ease the sudden tension. 'I get why, but I think she'll have to work hard to convince Sephy and me that it's the best thing to do. I suppose it's selfish to want to keep such a large place preserved as if nothing's changed. But there's so much of Dad in the place. And I don't see how she could be ready to deal with all of his things yet, which she'd have to if she chooses to sell,' she trailed off and indicated that they were turning into the next street.

'If she does sell where will Sephy and Daisy go?'

'I really don't know. Sephy loves it here and I don't think she'd want to move Daisy away from what she knows. Oh,' she stopped and put a hand on his arm. 'You're thinking Ryan is coming back and his daughter is moving away?'

'Really, it hadn't crossed my mind. If Sephy needed to move, neither Ryan nor I could stand in her way.' He put his hand in the small of her back to steer her safely around a couple of boys on skateboards and after they had passed them didn't see any reason to remove his hand. 'What about you? What is it you love about living where you are in London?'

She didn't answer straight away and he wondered if lately she'd been doing as much soul-searching as he had.

'It's close to the office,' she finally said with an elegant shrug.

'So basically KPC *is* London for you.' He reminded himself that there was more to her than work.

'I think so. I mean I know we have property everywhere, but I suppose, yes, I do think of KPC as always being in London.'

'And you must feel closer to your father there, too,' he said without thinking, seeing that enormous formal portrait of her father hanging near her office in his mind's eye.

'I—yes, I hadn't ever thought of it like that. Oh, this is us,' she said stopping outside a building and turning her head to stare down into her bag for long moments before reaching in to fish for the set of keys.

The minute Ethan stepped inside the building he knew it was right. The old dance studios would make a perfect Love Leisure, with only minimal remodelling needed. Ryan would be able to oversee the work while completing a training programme to manage the facilities.

'There's parking to the rear of the premises too,' Nora said, smiling her agreement at him as if he'd mentioned taking the place on immediately, out loud.

He nodded and started wandering around.

'Um, I'll pop next door for coffees while you take a proper look around.'

'Great. Thanks.' He headed over to a set of double doors that took him through to an office area.

By the time she came back, Ethan was sitting on top of a wood countertop that looked as though it had once housed a cash register and merchandise.

She set the cardboard tray down between them and sprang up onto the counter to sit beside him, having obviously used the time away from him to shore up her defences and make sure that ball of grief was firmly shoved back down and out of the way for today.

'I think you should keep the exposed brickwork as a feature,' she said lifting her coffee from the tray.

'And how did you know I was thinking that?'

Her eyes sparkled. 'Ah. I see love in your eyes, Ethan Love.'

Ethan blinked as the room shrunk down, until all he was aware of was he and Nora sitting atop a dusty wooden countertop, staring into each other's eyes. He felt as if he'd walked into a lamp post. Images rushed at him—flashes of living in one place and coming home to the same person every day. Images that didn't exacerbate the restlessness in him, but actually calmed it.

'Love for this building, that is,' Nora clarified, her eyes transforming into huge round saucers.

Ethan cleared his throat. 'I knew that. It is kind of perfect, isn't it?' he said, unable to tear his eyes from hers. Then, because he couldn't help acknowledge it, he said, 'Are you blushing, Nora?'

'Absolutely not,' she quipped. 'Drink your coffee.'

He smiled and did as he was told and they sat in companionable silence watching the world go by, until eventually, Nora asked, 'Do you think you'll ever reach the stage in your work where you'll think you've done enough?'

'In my line of work there is always going to be somewhere new to go.' Ethan took a swift glug of his coffee. Huh. He'd given his cop-out answer. The one he'd always told himself before he'd drawn the conclusions he had when sitting amongst the rubble of that collapsed building. He thought about the report he was waiting on. Hopefully he'd get the go-ahead to go back to Italy and finish up what he had started. Before he made the commitment to be in the field less, he wanted to know he'd fulfilled his promise to Pietro.

As if she knew that he had only given a stock answer, she prodded, 'But say *you'd* reached the point where you felt you'd done enough. What would you do then?'

'I guess I'd settle back into running Love Leisure full time.' He couldn't see himself never going back into the field, but he could see himself getting more involved with his business.

'But what about the staff you have doing that for you at the moment? What would happen to them?'

'I don't neglect my business responsibilities, Nora. You know better than anyone you can always find ways to improve and expand if the business model is sound. There'd be enough work to go round. My staff are rewarded for what they help the company achieve in my name while I'm elsewhere.'

'But what if Ryan decided he wanted to aim for the top at Love Leisure?'

'You really have a thing about "what ifs" don't you?' he couldn't help teasing. 'What if Ryan wanted to run Love Leisure? Well, then I guess I'll be damned proud of him and find myself something else to do.'

'You really think it's easy to change the course of your life.'

'Isn't that what your brother did?'

She frowned and then there was an imperceptible incline to her head to show she'd registered and accepted what he'd said.

'I don't think it would be easy, no,' he continued. 'But I've seen people's lives change in the course of one singular event and I've seen people *have* to change the course of their lives. It's what you do to survive. Anything else isn't really living.'

He thought back to how he'd asked her about what she'd be doing if she didn't have KPC and how she'd maybe lied. He thought of the intimacy they'd shared since and he held his breath when he asked again, 'What would you do if you didn't have KPC?'

Nora turned to slowly watch him, as if trying desperately to determine whether putting voice to her thoughts would somehow pass a point of no return. Then, licking her lips, she drew breath and whispered, 'You know when you want something so badly… that you never think about what you'll do when you get it?'

He put down his coffee. Yeah. He knew about that. Knew that, for all the words he'd said to her about changing your life, sometimes you never got around to actually doing that. Until you were holed up in a building for a few hours and forced to face yourself.

'Well, now I've got KPC all to myself and I'm not sure I have the emotional energy to find out.'

His heart swelled at her honesty. 'I think you do. I see it bubbling away inside you, right under the surface. I think you think that great big ball you're carrying around inside is *all* grief, but it isn't. You keep suppressing everything, it's never going to go away. You do know that, right?'

Nora swung her legs out in front of her a couple of times and frowned as her finger stole out to worry the corner of the cardboard drinks carrier.

Watching her reminded him of his parents and how difficult they too found it to express themselves emotionally.

But then he remembered that last night, with him, she hadn't found it difficult to express herself emotionally at all. He realised it wasn't that she found it difficult. It was that she was afraid she wouldn't be able to stop emoting once she'd started. Helping her deal with that before he left—making sure she had an outlet— would be a privilege. A small thing he could do to help.

'A big part of grief is all about anger and I know you've probably heard this before but that's because it's actually true—it's okay to still be grieving,' he told her.

'I know. And I have grieved,' she insisted again, then paused, 'all right am *still* grieving. But the bloody thing never comes at me in any logical way. Just when I think I've accepted…it turns out I haven't. And I miss him, okay?' She turned to look up at him, her eyes now enormous liquid pools. 'I miss my dad, Ethan.'

Ethan wanted to touch her. Acknowledge her pain. Wanted to automatically take some of it away from her and make it better straight away. He was used to providing the basics for people in need. Water, food, shelter. What could he give her to help her, the same way she had helped him?

Her hand was still busy picking at the cardboard and slowly he reached out and gently stopped her movements. She turned her palm upwards and linked her fingers with his.

'This isn't how I thought it would be,' she said with a sigh. 'I

151

mean, I thought I'd started grieving for him when the doctors told us there wasn't any more they could do. But I wasn't grieving. I was too busy...*hoping, fighting, praying.*'

Of course she had been.

'Now I feel so—' she shrugged her shoulders unable to speak, but he thought he knew.

She was feeling tired and empty.

Angry.

Hopeless.

Ethan heard Nora's frustrated 'Aaargh,' as she swiped at the couple of tears that had escaped and dropped her head onto his shoulder. 'I—can we not do this, please? Can you not be so damned accepting and nice and logical? It's turning me into a right mess. I was doing much better when I wasn't sure I liked you.'

He chuckled.

'It's just that we have to go meet Sephy and Daisy and I don't want to be—I can't be like this with them. Sephy's my baby sister. I don't want her to feel like I can't cope with all this.'

'Okay,' he said kissing the top of her head before jumping down off the countertop to face her. 'It will get better though. In time. You'll be back to feeling in control at KPC and loving it.'

Standing in front of her with her sat up on the countertop, her eyes were level with his and he could see how hard it was for her to trust in a process she couldn't see. She was wondering if she ever *would* love KPC again now that she was finally admitting out loud how completely on her own with it she felt.

'So where do I sign to get this building, then?' he asked wanting to lighten the mood for her.

Her smile held a note of relief and gratitude as she sniffed and jumped down off the counter. Rooting around in her bag, she pulled out her phone. 'How about I make the call and you speak to the agent? Then, we can stop by Sephy's for lunch.'

'Nora,' Ethan stopped her, 'something else that's—' he broke off, searching for the right words. 'I know I said I wouldn't let you pretend last night never happened, but I meant I wouldn't let you pretend with me. How do you want to play it with Sephy?'

'Oh,' she blushed again and he forbade himself to reach down and kiss her. The last thing she probably wanted was to turn up at Sephy's all ruffled up. 'Um, it might be awkward for you being Ryan's brother and everything.'

'I'm fine, but it's up to you.'

'Then let's not mention it, I'm pretty sure she won't notice anyway.'

Chapter Eleven

Sephy sidled up to where Nora was standing in front of the kitchen window and peered down at the scene before them. 'Oh. My. God. My child is completely obsessed with wellie-wanging. I don't get where I've gone wrong. What's to like about throwing a boot around a field like that?'

Nora watched while Ethan patiently helped Daisy improve her aim. He looked like an absolute giant next to the little girl, but he was so gentle and so good with her. Nora didn't even realise a wistful sigh had escaped her until Sephy bumped against her hip and asked her if she was okay.

'Of course,' she murmured, reining in all the warm and fuzzy emotions. 'Looking at Daisy, though, you might want to consider that there's a streak of shoe-fetish running through the family.'

'Great! Sometimes I worry about the example we're setting her, what with you obsessed with shoes and me obsessed with making underwear.'

'Lingerie,' Nora automatically corrected. Sephy had always played at designing gossamer-gorgeous lingerie, but in the last few months she'd really stepped it up a gear and got serious. For once Sephy didn't argue with her correction and Nora was pleased: Sephy deserved to value herself more.

Looking back out of the window, she marvelled at how visible the King genes were. Even if Daisy didn't have the same jet-black hair, from this distance Nora could see a stubborn lift to Daisy's chin that made her smile in recognition. 'Ooh, what if it's not the wellie-wanging, but more that she's fiercely competitive?' Turning to offer Sephy a mock-confused frown, she asked innocently, 'Wow! Who in our family could she possibly resemble?'

Sephy shuddered and rolled her eyes. 'That would be all of us, then.'

A couple of minutes passed and then Nora felt another not-so-subtle bump against her hip and turned to look at her sister's outrageous smirk. 'By the way, I've decided on a name for the collection.'

'That's great,' Nora said.

'Uh-huh. It came to me as soon as you walked through the front door earlier. I'm thinking,' Sephy spread her hands in a caption, "Nora Gets Some." has a nice ring to, hey—' She broke off to clasp the arm that Nora swiped at, unable to keep the grin off her face.

'It's really that obvious?' Nora asked aghast.

'Oh, it's only shining out of your every pore.' She laughed again when Nora's mouth dropped open. 'Relax. It's probably only obvious because it's been a while for me and I'm completely jealous.'

Nora sobered as she remembered something Ethan had mentioned. Turning to stare back out of the window, she said, 'Sephy, did you ever want a shot at KPC and feel that when Jared left you didn't even get a look in?'

'No, don't be silly. Trust me, me and KPC were never going to fall in love.'

Nora felt an immediate flood of relief. It was hard enough to reconcile the guilt over Jared not being given KPC, regardless of her knowing he had his own business in New York, without now worrying that she'd stomped all over her sister's dreams as well. She had thought she'd accepted that Jared didn't blame her and in fact admired her for going after what she had wanted when he left, but lately every time she'd started questioning herself she revisited that as well.

'But there were a few years after Jared left,' Sephy said slowly, 'when I was furiously jealous that you and Dad had such a good relationship.'

A few years?

Nora reached out to rub one of the petals from the row of African violets that Sephy kept in pretty blue pots on the window-sill. A few years was a long time. She remembered that that was when Sephy had started hanging around with Ryan and going out of her way to shock. No doubt hoping their father would just notice her.

Nora thought about what Ethan had said about his parents. She was beginning to understand how Ryan and Sephy must have felt like two peas in a pod as they ran around town partying, feeling that everyone in their families was disinterested.

Jeremy King's way of noticing the change in his daughter had been to ignore Sephy's bad behaviour completely, right up until it reached the stage where it started impinging on the family's standing in the town. Their relationship had gone downhill from that point on and had only got better when Daisy had been born.

Nora felt her insides pull in tight. If only their father had been less good at business and less bad at communicating with his children. Jared wouldn't have felt he had no option but to leave. Sephy wouldn't have felt she had no option but to seek out atten-tion and she wouldn't have felt such pressure to chase something she no longer knew whether she wanted or not.

'I'm so incredibly, disgustingly, angry at Dad, Sephy,' Nora whispered, shaking her head helplessly.

There. She'd said it.

Perhaps it would get easier to say, but right now her mouth felt dry with the guilt of it and her stomach queasy from the energy that anger created. 'And it feels so disrespectful. Out of the three of us, I thought I was the one who understood him best, but

sometimes the way he chose to deal with us by ignoring us...
Why am I feeling it all now? Why not then?'

'Sometimes I used to think my anger would swallow me up,'
Sephy said in a rush, 'not so much now, though. When I read my
letter I was—God, Nora, it was worse than anger. I think it was
hate.' Her hand came up to cover her mouth as if to deny the
words that had left her lips but then she took a big, shaky breath
and smiled. 'But thank God for Daisy, because in not wanting her
to see her own mother filled up with such a negative emotion
I had to pull myself together pretty quickly and in the process
I realised I didn't really hate him at all. What I hated was that
what he said in his letter to me was true and for my own good,
and for Daisy's good. He was who he was. A businessman first;
a husband and father second. And, hey, maybe some of the King
business skills rubbed off on me after all, because I'm telling you
this—I'm going to make a success of my lingerie line. I have all
these plans, Nora. Great big plans and Luke's going to help me.
I just have to find a way to get him to offer.'

Once upon a time Nora had lived and breathed plans for KPC
and then she caught the look in her sister's eye. The same look that
had probably been in her own eyes every time she'd told Ethan
she didn't need his help. 'You can't simply ask Luke to help you?'
she asked softly, thinking how similar they were at times.

Sephy studied her manicure carefully. 'I really don't think I can.'

Nora and Ethan had been so personal with each other in such
a short space of time. Was she wrong to trust in that, then? Sephy
and Luke had known each other at least a year and were good
enough friends that he was around more often than he wasn't. If
Sephy couldn't swallow her pride and ask him for help, what the
hell was Nora doing soaking up Ethan's.

As if Sephy could sense her spiralling thoughts she grabbed
Nora in a fierce, quick hug and said, 'Enjoy Ethan, Nora. Neither
of you are looking to make this something it isn't, are you?'

Nora shook her head.

'No harm, no foul, then,' Sephy said easily.

But what if…

'So, come on,' Sephy cajoled, 'While he's out-of-the-way dish. What's he like in bed?'

'Seraphina King, I am so not going to answer that,' Nora said, with her nose in the air.

'Please,' came the reply with a full-on begging note. 'Just a few details.' She leant forward and practically pressed her nose up against the glass. 'He's really built—my eyes nearly popped out of my head when I saw him in the robe I had to lend him. Tell me he knows what to do with all that muscle? Tell me *you* knew what to do with it.'

Nora took a hasty step back when Ethan suddenly turned to stare up at the window and wave to them both.

'Are you blushing?' Sephy asked in delight. 'Hey,' Sephy snapped her fingers in Nora's dreamy face, 'Earth to Nora? Oh my God, I love it—your face is definitely saying that Ethan Love is incredibly good and deliciously bad.'

Nora burst out laughing and Sephy joined in.

'Oh, I've missed having a giggle with my sister,' Sephy sighed. 'And you deserve to have some fun.'

'That's all it is,' Nora felt impelled to say out loud once again. 'A bit of simple fun.' She knew the things that Ethan and she had talked about weren't simple or necessarily fun but somehow they went with how they'd been with each other. He made talking so easy.

As long as they both understood the boundaries, she hoped that Sephy was right. No foul, no harm.

She didn't have time to hurt over anything else.

'I keep hoping I'll get to hook up with one of Jared's friends when we all go out for the wedding in a few months,' Sephy said as she nudged Nora in the ribs, 'Perhaps my big sister might do some babysitting for me.'

Oh.

Jared and Amanda's wedding.

'Of course I will,' she said but inside all she was suddenly thinking was that Ethan would be long gone by then.

She probably wouldn't even know where he was.

She wondered if they would keep in touch, maybe email or text each other once in a while. Would he ever want to stop over and see her when he was back in town? And what would happen the first time he came back to visit Ryan? Would he stop off and see Sephy and Daisy too?

What if he didn't want to really see her again after this thing, whatever it was, had run its course? She'd be in London, knowing that they were all meeting up.

It would all be so awkward.

For her, at least.

Best not to spoil whatever they were doing with questions, though.

Best not force the issue.

***

Nora stood in front of her custom-designed shoe racks dressed only in her underwear. Her toes squeezed in pleasure against the luxurious deep-piled cream carpet as she thought about which pair of shoes to wear for meeting Ethan.

Most women would probably decide what outfit to wear before they chose matching shoes, but for Nora it was always going to be about the shoes first—all the lovely shoes that helped transform her into the best version of herself.

In the perfect pair of shoes she could walk into a meeting, any meeting, with her confidence brimming.

Not that she needed confidence when she met with Ethan. She smiled a private smile. No, what she probably needed was a little self-restraint.

Something he made nigh on impossible with one heat-filled look from his baby-blues as he spied whichever shoes she was wearing and she turned to putty.

The putty-like effect had been present for three weeks now.

Three weeks of fun-filled, heart-swelling, body-craving hasty assignations in between work meetings.

Then there were all the nights where they ended up back at her apartment and with him staying until she left for work the next morning. Some nights she watched him sleeping, her heart full that he could now. But then she would sneak out to the lounge to do some work or watch some mindless TV. Anything to stop her wondering about where he might be needed next and when that might be. In those few spare minutes between work and being with him, it was easy to put off worrying about how she'd got amazingly proficient at shuffling her work to meet up with him.

It hadn't taken her long to realise that she had been so busy looking backwards to what had happened in her family; she had forgotten the restorative powers of looking forward to something. And she had started looking forward to being with Ethan over most things.

Spotting her new Jimmy Choo flame-coloured suede and metallic-strap sandals, she reached out. She could team them with…a coat, because it wasn't the warm end of spring quite yet.

Her head tipped to the side as she analysed the many etiquette rules she'd be breaking if she walked around a house that Ethan had potentially sourced for Ryan, with an estate agent at their side and her knowing that all she was wearing was a coat and a pair of Jimmy Choo shoes. Then she thought about what Ethan would think when he realised and where they could go afterwards so that he could peel the coat off her.

Hardly house-viewing attire, but that wasn't the point.

Halfway to bending down to put on one of the sexy sandals, Nora sprang straight back up, shocked to her core.

What the hell was she thinking—the house-viewing was *so* the point of their meeting.

This thing with Ethan was getting way out of hand.

Okay the sex between them was in a whole-other-stratosphere good, but they talked as well—sometimes before, during and after. She liked that they did that. Felt that it was part of the healing-each-other journey that they were on.

But once Ethan had found the right place for his brother to live in, what would really be left to hold him here. Surely he'd head off to wherever the world needed him to be.

He'd go and she'd be left with nothing but memories of the two of them together to fuel the gaps between meetings at work. What would work feel like then? Was she only starting to enjoy it again because it wasn't her sole focus?

Now she wished she'd put a few barriers in place. Told Ethan even one of the times he'd suggested meeting up that she wasn't free.

She was reminded of all the times she'd met with Steve, her ex, fitting him in quickly between meetings and thinking that she liked that about their relationship, that it made it work.

But it wasn't what made their relationship work.

Nora chewed down hard on her lip as realisation hit hard.

Steve had been right: She *had* been married to her job back then. And the relationship had suffered.

Now enjoying the times she and Ethan met up, for the first time in her life work was taking second-place. And when Ethan left, what if KPC didn't fill the hole?

Nora went cold all over and then the uncertainty came to twist up her insides so that she thought she was going to be sick.

This was bad. Really bad.

Three weeks grace and now returning to all the hateful second-guessing felt worse than it ever had before.

Catching herself in the mirror, she despised the sea of vulnerability in her eyes—would do anything to rid herself of that... and then she stopped.

Hang on a minute, why am I getting all weirded-out? Ethan and I aren't even in a relationship.

Breathing became a little easier.

That big ball of churning emotion sat itself back down inside her because, hey, if she didn't have a relationship with Ethan then she was completely entitled to arrange to meet him knowing they were going to have sex as soon as they were on their own.

That's what you did when you were doing simple fun.

It was all good.

Nothing to see here. Guilt—move right along.

Still.

Nora returned the shoes to the shoe rack.

The notion that she was free to make her and Ethan only about sex didn't sit quite right with her.

Perhaps she should test herself a little. Just to check she wasn't so enslaved to being in his arms that she couldn't be in his company and survive being out of them for any length of time.

What she needed was a pair of shoes that would help her make that point.

***

'I'm sure she'll be here in a minute,' Ethan said to the estate agent as he glanced up the street hoping to see her car.

He tried to get a handle on whether it was that he was missing her or whether it was that he was worried about her. He flicked the sleeve of his jacket to glance at his watch. She wasn't even ten minutes late.

Which meant it was ridiculous to be missing her *or* worrying.

Okay, he could admit to himself that he wanted to get the house tour over with.

He needed to be alone with Nora so that he could talk to her about the email he'd received. God, the spike in his heart-rate when he'd spied the risk assessment report from the charity sitting in his email inbox. Oh, he might have spent weeks telling himself he couldn't affect the outcome of the report. That he'd given his statement and was confident he'd be cleared—that there would be no big black mark put against his record in the job. But all the time, eating away at him, had been the wait for judgement.

For a few seconds staring at his computer screen he'd considered putting himself through some more waiting. Just so he got to spend some more time with Nora before the results of the report came between them. Postponing finding out was simply hiding from his future, though, wasn't it? Trapped in that building in Italy he'd decided he was through doing that.

So he'd opened the document and read the report over and over until it had sunk in—the risk assessment the charity had carried out had, thank God, cleared him of any recklessness. He was free to return to work on the condition he accept his error in judgment about going into the building without notifying anyone first.

Being hauled up for breaking protocol and sent home before he could see that little boy reach his parents had been incredibly hard, but now he was free to return to Italy and check for himself that Pietro had made it back to them. He was also free to work with his team knowing no one thought he'd go maverick on them.

That his work reputation was clear and untainted meant everything to him. Now he could finish what he'd started, his record blemish-free. He was going back to northern Italy tomorrow to change the course of his life.

Being trapped in that building had forced him to face himself and what he wanted out of life. In promising Pietro he'd make sure he re-united him with his parents, he'd realised that if something happened to *him*, his own family would barely know him. Travelling and the type of work he did was such an easy excuse not to visit and the freedom his parents had always given their sons made it even easier to let each other slip through their fingers. Dutiful birthday cards and Christmas phone calls had become the family's limit.

But the fear of not surviving that aftershock had been acute. Picturing his parents and brother having to learn about him through friends and colleagues had felt ridiculously selfish and stupid. Why not get to know them and let them know him. Form a new and adult impression.

When they'd sent a cheque for Ryan's rehab he'd torn it up and told himself he wouldn't push for too much too soon, but the reality was he'd used the outcome of the report hanging over him to restrict how far we was willing to put himself out there. His fear they'd never get him, or that he'd never get them, had made its way to the forefront of his mind.

He didn't have that excuse any more. He'd promised himself he'd get Pietro out and then find a way to start reconnecting with his family and this time as soon as he'd finished helping in Italy, that was what he was going to do.

It was going to be hard letting the work that had driven him for years take more of a back seat, but the situation with Pietro had brought home the urgency of saving his own family relationships. And then he'd met Nora...

He couldn't imagine her not being in his life—him not being in hers. He had tried so hard to keep reminding them that being together was only temporary. He hadn't wanted to over-promise and have to break his word, but in truth these past three weeks had felt like a glimpse of something so special, he'd be a fool not to pursue it. Being holed up in that building had reset his thinking and now he could see his future opening up again in front of him. He wanted to ask her whether he'd have something to come back to when he returned.

Something with her.

A chance was all he needed.

But would she think what they had was worth trying to turn into something more?

She'd said she couldn't imagine him being nervous and he'd

laughed it off, but he was nervous now, he thought, tapping the rolled-up house particulars against his thigh as he walked up and down outside the house.

He glanced down the road once more and was relieved to find her pulling in behind the estate agent's vehicle.

She smiled when she got out of the car and his heart did a funny little tumbling thing that had his hand coming up subconsciously to his chest in a rubbing movement.

He jogged down the driveway to greet her. His first instinct was to pull her in close and lean down for a kiss because it had been hours since he'd put his lips on her, but he managed to check himself at the last instant when she gave him a quick, shy frown before her gaze moved to take in the estate agent.

Note to self: no PDAs, Ethan.

The small rejection stung but he shook it off and introduced her to the agent, who was going to show them around the modern town house.

The guy went straight into sales spiel as he let them both into the house, '...so come in, come in. Let's see, the property came on the market three weeks ago. Downstairs is a little larger than the average house in this area due to the extension. Upstairs, three bedrooms. En-suite to master, a spare room and nursery...'

Nora came to a sudden stop in front of him and whipped her head around to meet Ethan's amused gaze. She had gone delightfully pink and it occurred to him that he had neglected to tell the estate agent that he was looking at the house for his brother, not for him.

'Do you know if there are any good schools in the area?' he asked and smiled harder when Nora's mouth dropped open.

'I believe there's one within walking distance.' The man turned to look at Nora and when his gaze slid down to her stomach and Ethan saw her go pale he realised he might have gone too far. Perhaps it hadn't occurred to her that the estate agent could have assumed it was the two of them looking at the house with a view to buying it for themselves. Perhaps she thought Ryan and his girlfriend were thinking of having a baby and felt weird about that because of Ryan's non-relationship with Daisy.

She got quieter and quieter as the tour of the house progressed until finally the estate agent said he had some calls to make and would wait in his car to give them a chance to look around on their own.

'Alone at last,' Ethan muttered when they were left in the lounge facing each other.

Nora frowned and he wished to hell he knew what she was thinking.

'What do you think of the place, then?' he asked.

She looked around the living room. 'I think it's lovely.' And then slowly she brought her gaze back to study him, 'Ethan, are you planning on buying this house for Ryan?'

He couldn't help himself; at the note of censure in her tone he felt his jaw go tight. 'What's the matter, don't you think I can afford it?'

'I am quite sure you can. But what if—'

'Go on,' he said, aware that his voice lacked a certain degree of patience because he'd had other more important thoughts in his head and with one question she'd managed to derail him and bring him back down to earth. 'What if, what?'

She shook her head as if she didn't know where to start. 'I just wonder if you're in danger of fixing a little too much in his life, for him. I know you mean well, but your need to wade in to the rescue—'

'He phoned me, not the other way around,' he said, his voice tight and defensive.

'But Ethan what if further down the line he starts to resent everything you've done?'

'I don't want Ryan to have to deal with any financial pressures. Surely you agree that's important, given the circumstances.'

'But to buy him a house… Why not rent something for him

166

for a while? Because the first time you buy a house,' she looked down and appeared to be choosing her words carefully and when she looked up her face was full of concern, 'well, it should be for yourself.'

Ethan felt emotion flood him as he stood in front of her. He couldn't answer her any other way except to say that, yes, in an ideal world, his first property should be for him—or the two of them. What would she say if he threw that out there? It's what he had been thinking as he'd walked around this house with her. Not that he'd want this particular property, but he'd rushed full-speed ahead to thinking that finding one with her wouldn't be so scary at all. Would actually be kind of a fun adventure.

Which was all the ways wrong because he was supposed to be asking her for a chance with him.

Not scaring the living daylights out of her by asking for too much too soon.

It was one thing to decide to change your lifestyle, but he knew the hardest bit was going to be conquering his fear that he'd try staying in one place and wouldn't like it, or worse, wouldn't be able to cut it. What if the restlessness he felt as an adult was trying to tell him he wasn't built to stay in one place because he was too like his parents? What if he shouldn't ask her for a chance because it might lead to this and he'd screw it all up?

He scraped his hand over the back of his head in frustrated uncertainty. God, she was getting him hooked on all the what-if's in life now.

'I need to do this for Ryan,' he told her.

'You need to buy him a house?' she asked, incredulous.

It was more what the house represented. A fresh start. A solid foundation. Permanency. 'I should have tried harder to help him when we were younger. It didn't take a genius to work out he was rebelling against all the constant moving. I left him floundering and I knew it. As much as he didn't want help I should have spoken up quicker, should have kept speaking up.' Shouldn't have felt his parents thought he was judging them for their lack of parenting skills and punishing him back for his judgement by not listening to him.

Nora automatically looked contrite. 'It's not your fault he's made some mistakes. You're not responsible for him, Ethan. He is. I guarantee you that that's what he's learning right now in rehab. You're going to have to prepare yourself for him wanting to practise what he's learning.' She stepped towards him. 'Ryan is lucky to have you as a big brother, but I realised with Sephy that it's better to be on their side than on their case. One thing a younger sibling hates is feeling as if they can't be trusted to run their own lives.'

Ethan wondered if when he stopped doing the response team-work, he'd still feel he was being judged for not doing enough and then felt a warning tingle at the top of his spine. What if, in stopping sinking his energies into response teamwork the character trait became even more pronounced? 'All right, I'll make sure that he and I work out a deal for further down the line.' His hand shot out to pull her into his arms because he didn't want to think any more. Didn't want to worry that actually now he wasn't sure what he had to offer her. 'You're very sexy when you're being wise,' he whispered, nuzzling the hair away from her ear to add a kiss, 'and giving advice,' his added, sliding his lips down the smooth line of her throat. He loved that she released a small moan and brought her hands up to sweep up his chest, over his shoulders and into his hair.

He lifted his mouth to find her lips. She responded immediately, her tongue sliding out to meet his, her body pressing itself as close as she could get and within seconds he was wanting to find the nearest available surface to place her on or push her up against. He had moved her halfway across the room before he remembered where he was and what he had intended the evening to be about.

Breaking the kiss, he rested his forehead against hers, tempted beyond reason to go back to kissing her when he realised her breathing was every bit as unsteady as his.

Reining himself in, he said, 'I'm thinking we should go back to the hotel—'

'The hotel? Not my place?'

If they went back to her place, and he laid himself on the line, in her home and she didn't want that... But if they had dinner at the hotel restaurant, he'd be in public and have less chance of getting distracted by being alone with her. He wanted to know one way or another before he left for northern Italy. 'I was actually thinking we could have a lazy dinner in the restaurant, maybe talk about the house some more and then talk about some other things.'

'Oh,' she stiffened in his arms and his nerves quadrupled. 'I'm not dressed for the restaurant.'

He glanced down to what she was wearing and finally figured out why she hadn't seemed as tall as usual. She was wearing flats not heels. For once he was kind of glad that she wasn't wearing shoes that frazzled his brain. It would make it much easier to ask her for that chance.

Chapter Twelve

Nora placed a forkful of Michelin-star food in her mouth and chewed, barely aware of what she was eating. Here she was sitting at a corner table of the Grand Hotel's restaurant dressed in a casual top, skinny jeans…and pristine white plimsolls.

But this is what happened when the maitre d' recognised you, or recognised your money at any rate, and made a dress-code exception.

This was not a plimsoll establishment.

Her apartment was.

That house she and Ethan had toured had been.

But this…was not.

The journey back in the car had been filled with small talk—the kind of talking they'd never had to resort to and so it had been hard and unfamiliar and stilted.

A sharp and stabbing painful reminder that Nora had been living on borrowed time with Ethan.

She'd stupidly walked around that house with him and each step she'd taken had come with an inner voice screaming at her that this was the more that she wanted.

A life with Ethan.

God! What was wrong with her? How could she have been stupid—so greedy, to have taken something that was supposed to be simple fun and want it to mean more.

It was all Ethan's fault.

All this time he'd been making her feel again—and all this time what had he been feeling?

She was pretty sure all he'd been feeling was exactly what they had agreed to.

A stopover.

Why else would he bring her to his hotel, if not to end it because he was leaving to return to his job?

Because here wasn't personal. Here was public and simple and fun.

'How's your risotto?' Ethan asked.

Nora glanced down to her plate of food. She'd ordered the first thing off the menu that she'd seen because her mind had been racing too much to concentrate on something as simple as food.

'It's lovely,' she answered flatly. She looked over at his plate, 'How's your lamb?'

'It's good,' he answered, cutting himself another piece.

Nora's stomach sank.

For a man who wanted to talk he was being very quiet.

For once she didn't get annoyed with herself for not wanting to force the issue. She didn't want to hear what he had to say.

She'd replayed everything he'd said to her from their conversation at the house to the drive here and all through the meal. He'd liked the house because it was the last piece of the puzzle to sorting everything out for Ryan before he left. He'd had her in his arms and glanced down at her shoes and instead of making a plan to rip each other's clothes off he'd made a plan to talk to her—to let her down gently.

Nora moved her feet under the table and felt the rubber soles of her plimsolls drag against the expensive parquetry flooring.

It was all so embarrassing. There she'd been putting on shoes to test them both a little—to demonstrate she didn't want to think of them only being about sex and all the while he'd been planning on telling her their time together was at an end.

If she'd known tonight was going to be about goodbye she'd have put on her favourite Louboutins.

She put another mouthful of food in her mouth and tried to swallow, looked across at Ethan and saw him fumble his fork. Her gentle giant was uncomfortable and in spite of herself her heart went out to him. He was essentially a good man, a compassionate man, a fair man, and she hated that he might be struggling to tell her because he was worried she was too fragile to hear him. She winced. It wasn't like she hadn't poured her heart out to him and shown him how she struggled keeping her emotions under control.

Suddenly she didn't want his last impressions of her to be weak, feeble or needy.

Straightening her spine she told herself that if this was going to be goodbye, she was going to go out with her head held high. She'd hear his words and she'd let him know that she understood that all good things came to an end. That she had always known that this was temporary. A little healing and a lot fun. Simple.

'I'm going to drive down to see Ryan early tomorrow morning,' Ethan said breaking into her thoughts.

'To go over everything?'

'Yeah.'

'That's…great.' Because they were friends now and she knew it was going to be difficult for him seeing Ryan and because she was pathetic and wanted a tiny bit more time with him, she said, 'I could come with you if you like.'

'Thanks but I think it would be better if I went on my own this—'

'Of course,' she interrupted realising she'd just gone against everything she was resolved to do. She was supposed to be making this easy not difficult. Clean break not clingy. She felt his intense regard and she lowered her eyes to the table, too cowardly to let him see how hard it was going to be to let him go.

This was awful.

Mentally she pictured her Louboutins at the end of her feet.

'Nora, I—' Ethan stopped, picked up his wine glass and took a gulp.

Oh, God, here it came. She breathed in and with everything inside her, prepared to end their time together in a blaze of glory not a puff of a 'thank you' speech.

'Ethan,' Nora cut him off, leant forward and said, her voice as clear as a bell, 'Take me upstairs to your room and make love with me.'

Nora opened her eyes as Ethan crept out of the bed and headed for the shower. She waited until she heard the water splash against marble and glass and then flopped over onto her back. Her hand swiped at a couple of tears that leaked out.

Enough with the tears, Leonora King.

Just because it had been the most beautiful night ever.

Just because with every caress of his hands, every kiss of his lips and every moan he'd elicited from her she'd wanted it not to be goodbye.

Not everybody got to have everything.

And she certainly wasn't going to ask everything of a man she'd only known for weeks. It was ridiculous to even contemplate. Forcing an issue never won the prize. They'd run their course. Run out of time.

Besides, she had more than some people had.

She had KPC.

She didn't need more.

She didn't need him.

What she needed to do was reinvest herself wholly in her company. Make up for the inches of neglect that had started creeping in. That would give her something to focus on.

Rising from the bed, she looked around for her clothes. They were tangled up with Ethan's and strewn over the floor, the dressing table and the bed.

173

Evidence of how intertwined they had become.

She'd asked him not to let her fall too hard and hadn't even realised she already had.

As she tugged on her jeans and fastened the button at the back of her jumper more tears threatened to fall. That great big ball of emotion she'd kept shoving back down inside of her felt as if it was going to break free of her any minute and in order to survive she was going to have to let it—but first she had to get out of this room.

What would he think when he came out of the shower to find her gone? Pride made her question whether she should at least leave him a note. Tell him that she was walking, not running, and thank him for…she squeezed her eyes shut to stem the tears and when she felt steadier opened them to scan the room's surfaces for a pen. Her eyes alighted instead on his laptop as it charged on his dressing table. She flipped the lid up but then paused. What did she say? How did she find the words?

No. She couldn't do it.

She was sitting at the dressing table tying her shoelace when the bathroom door opened and Ethan strode out.

Bloody plimsolls. She was so throwing them in the bin when she got home. If she'd been wearing heels she could have slipped her feet into them and been out of there already. She wouldn't have had to hear the speech, feel the pity, pretend it didn't matter.

'Hey, I was thinking about ordering some breakfast for us,' Ethan said, stopping and frowning when he noticed her fully dressed and doing up her shoes.Lord, she lowered her head so that he couldn't see the tear-tracks.

'I'm good, thanks,' she said, her voice a sort of muffled whisper as she bent down and busied herself tying her other shoe.

'You don't sound it,' he said hesitantly.

Her head came up and she blew a strand of hair out of her eyes. 'I'm in a hurry that's all.'

'A hurry? We have a bit of time yet.'

'We really don't, Ethan,' she said standing up and preparing to leave before she had her meltdown in front of him.

Strong. That's what she'd promised herself in the hours before dawn. She would be strong and she would leave and she would get herself home before she released the emotion. She wouldn't let him see that although he'd been honest with her and told her that their being together could only be temporary, she'd made it awkwardly into something more in her head.

'What the hell?' Ethan bit out, obviously realising she had been planning on leaving without so much as a reciprocal 'so long and thanks for all the memories'. 'You were going to leave without saying goodbye?'

She watched his gaze flicker uncertainly to the laptop behind her, saw his abdominals pull in tight and felt herself go red at the brief flash of dread that entered his eyes. He reached around her and stabbed at a button to bring the screen to life. She stood there mortified. Not even able to turn and glance at the screen or Ethan's face to see how he felt about the fact that she hadn't even taken the time to type him a quick note. Instead she ordered herself not to look at him and catalogue what she'd be missing within minutes of leaving the hotel room. She shrugged her shoulders. 'I know you must have a lot to do before you set off.'

'My flight's not until two this afternoon.'

So he *was* leaving.

It was harder hearing the words than she had thought possible; like her head understood, but her heart had to hear it to really believe. Briefly she wondered whether he would have got around to actually telling her. If she'd managed to leave before he'd come out of the shower, what would he have done? Texted her?

Well, why wouldn't he, she supposed. They were only simple fun.

'Nora, I'm sorry. I meant to tell you about Italy last night but I—we got carried away.'

'That's all right. It's better this way, I think.'

He folded his arms across his chest. 'It is?'

She nodded, trying not to notice his biceps bulge. Trying not to remember how gently he had held her. 'Let's not make this awkward for each other. I imagine we'll bump into each other sometimes because of the family connection.'

Ethan stared at her for a long time, his expression inscrutable. 'So—that's it, then?' he finally said.

'I hope you have a safe trip.' She licked her lips. She was running out of words. Running out of breath. 'Thank you—'

Ethan barked out a laugh. 'Thank you? You make it sound like I was performing some sort of service.'

'Well, in a way, weren't you?' she asked softly, raising her gaze to his. 'Tell me. Tell me you didn't think you'd come along and bounce me out of myself. For fun. Because you could. Because of that ego of yours and that hero deal you have going on.'

He went pale beneath his natural tan and she cursed that she was making a hash of leaving. Hated that some of the anger was starting to shake loose. 'Hey, it's okay. I'm thanking you because amongst all the sex and talking it actually worked. I'm fixed now.'

'Is that what you really think?'

Her hand came up to rest between her breasts. As if she could staunch the flow of her heart bleeding.

She *knew* it.

Knew that apart from the simple fun he looked at her as something still in need of his fixing.

'What I think,' she said, pulling in a shaky breath and forcing a smile, 'is that we had fun together. You came here to achieve something very specific. You've done that. Your brother is getting himself fixed and you've fixed everything else for him. You were always going to go back to Italy afterwards, and then onto wherever else it is you're needed.'

'And I'm not needed here—that's what you're saying?'

He was wanted, yes. Needed, yes.

But not because she was needy or needing to be fixed.

Never those things.

She wanted him to stay because he *wanted* to, because he was choosing *her*. 'That's exactly what I'm saying,' she answered, picking up her scattering emotions and shoving them back inside of her any old way they would fit.

'Right. Well,' Ethan pushed his hair back with his hands and cleared his throat. 'In that case, thank you to you too. To think that I—' he broke off with a quick shake of his head. 'It's been an,' he seemed to search for the appropriate word, 'eye-opener,' he finished with and she felt the insult all the way down to her core.

She had to get out of here.

Right the hell now.

Striding to the door she put her hand on the handle to wrench it open, only to find Ethan's large palm slamming against the wood to prevent her leaving. She dragged air into her lungs and when his other hand reached out to stroke down the length of her hair it broke her heart he was so gentle. 'Nora, if you had asked me to stay—'

God. Nora closed her eyes. Did he want to stay? Did he want her after all? Had she misunderstood?

'—I would have said that I couldn't because I made a promise to somebody and I keep my promises.'

She couldn't speak. Of course he was the type of man who kept promises. Did he think it made her feel better to realise he had taken every care not to make her any?

'I would have come back for you though.'

Because he saw someone who needed his help. He'd come back to help her. She'd only been a promise he'd made to himself. A tear trickled down her cheek.

'But you were never going to ask me to stay, were you? You're too locked into your world and you already know I don't stay where I'm not needed.' Nora felt him lean a bit closer and his quiet, 'Take care of yourself, Princess,' was nearly more than she could bear.

You see, Nora. He doesn't see you as fearless.

He sees you as a worst-case scenario.

177

'You too,' she whispered.

His hand moved down to the door handle and she tore her hand away before it could close over hers. He opened the door and she flew through it.

The lift doors to Nora's penthouse apartment closed behind her. She let her bag slip off her shoulder as her fingers came up automatically to release the belt of her coat. On auto-pilot she moved through to her bedroom and walk-in wardrobe.

Her eyes lighted on her racks of shoes and absurdly she felt the first of the waves of emotion rise up.

She was glad she'd worn the flat plimsolls now. They'd been so much easier to run in. She only wished she could outrun the tidal wave about to hit her.

Sinking to the floor she hugged her knees in to her chest, bent to rest her head in her arms and waited for the sobbing to take effect.

How long she stayed like that for she didn't know, but she became confused when the tears didn't come, when the army of emotion didn't rise up inside her and revolt. Instead, she now felt strangely, uncomfortably, empty. It was as if someone had excavated the roiling ball of emotion in her, leaving her an empty shell.

Sighing, she got up from the floor, padded back through the apartment to where she'd left her bag and rifled through the contents for her phone.

There was no way she could go into work in this ghost-like state.

She found Fern's mobile number entry and pressed it. Fern answered on the first ring and for a second Nora forgot why she was phoning her and then she remembered.

'Fern. I'm going to work from home today.'

'No problem. You only had one meeting. I'll cancel it.'

When Nora didn't show any interest in who the meeting was with, Fern asked, 'Is everything okay?'

'Everything's fine. I'm just swamped,' she fibbed, not wanting to worry Fern. 'Can you try and only ring me if it's an emergency?'

'Sure thing, boss.'

'Bye then.'

Nora ended the call and tucking the phone into the pocket of her jumper, wandered over to the sofa, where she sat down and stared towards the windows. Not really seeing the view. Not really seeing anything.

Vaguely she remembered the last time she had felt like this.

The day her father had died.

What she was feeling was shock, then.

The first part of grieving.

With a huge sigh, her shoulders slumped and she blinked a couple of times to try and clear the dry, gritty feeling in her eyes. She was tired. Kind of exhausted. Slowly she stretched out on the sofa. Resting her face on her upturned palm she stared out of the windows some more until sleep finally came to claim her.

She woke up cold and confused. Fumbling for her phone, she pressed the menu screen to find out the time and saw that it was a little after two-thirty in the afternoon.

Ethan would be in the air.

On his way and out of her life.

She had to find some way to acknowledge it or she'd be as bad as she'd been when her father died. Only this time she didn't feel the responsibility of KPC as a draw to keep her going.

Hauling herself upright, she stood up and walked over to the kitchen area to fill the kettle. She needed tea and then she needed a plan.

Maybe she should watch a sad film—get some of the emotion out the way.

The kettle boiled and she reached for a mug and popped a herbal teabag in.

At least this time she recognised she couldn't go back to work like this. It was one thing to keep things going when the whole company was in shock and mourning the loss of her father.

How could she possibly let them see her grieving over the loss of what? Great sex and an almost-relationship?

She felt so stupid to have put herself in this position. As if she'd allowed the situation to sneak up on her and jeopardise all the progress she'd been making at KPC recently.

Before Ethan had appeared in her offices she'd been on course with her life. She'd known exactly what she needed to do to make things better for herself at KPC. To make the company better. To make her father proud. To fix the aching hole his loss had left behind.

She felt a little bubble of anger flutter against her breastbone.

Ethan had told her she was too locked into her world.

What the hell did that mean?

Had he thought she wouldn't be able to run KPC *and* have a relationship?

Unimaginative bastard!

Unimaginative *wrong* bastard!

Not that she had ever proved herself capable of having both, she realised, sipping her tea and becoming disappointed that the herbal tea leaves were doing nothing to quieten the now churning anger.

Yes, there had to be a King running KPC.

It was what her father had expected.

And she was the only one who had wanted it. She couldn't let him down.

That didn't mean she…

Her mobile rang, making her jump.

But she didn't even have to look at the screen to know it was psychic Sephy, the ringtone was enough. She couldn't face talking to her sister. She was too…she sniffed. Her vision blurred with unshed tears and she burnt her tongue on the boiling-hot tea.

The main phone on her desk rang.

She poked her burnt tongue out at it.

The answerphone clicked on.

'Pick up Nora,' Sephy said. 'I already know you're not at work because I spoke to Fern.'

180

There was a short silence and then a soft and sympathetic, utterly humiliating sounding, 'Ethan phoned me.'

Oh my God, he hadn't—please say he hadn't phoned her sister to tell her she needed checking up on or looking after. Actual air miles were between them now and still he was doing the helpful thing. The stupid and completely not-needed-hero thing.

'Norsies if you don't come to the phone right now I'm putting your niece on the line and she's going to cry if she asks for her Auntie Nora and gets nothing in—'

'Oh for God's sake, I'm here all right,' Nora said, snatching up the phone and pulling out her desk chair to plonk herself on. 'You shouldn't use your own child as blackmail, like that. It's not right,' she said grumpily.

'Norsies.'

'And don't call me that.' Why did everyone insist on calling her anything other than by her name? She remembered Ethan breathing the word "Princess" almost reverently into her ear as he moved inside of her and she closed her eyes in helplessness.

'Okay. Sorry. So.'

'Sephy I really am all right.'

'I thought you would be. It's, well, when Ethan rang me—'

'What did he say?'

'Only that he'd been to see Ryan and sorted out a lot of things with him and that Ryan would like to make contact before he moved down in a few weeks. He didn't want it to be a shock if I saw him around town. Wanted to give me a date so that I could be prepared. He sounded upset.'

'Ryan did? That doesn't bode well.' Nora quickly tried to marshal some strength so she could calculate whether or not she could juggle things at work to stay with Sephy for a couple of weeks when Ryan moved down to the area. She was due a fair bit of holiday.

'No. *Ethan* sounded upset—well, more angry, actually.'

'Angry? What does he have to be angry about?'

'I was kind of hoping you could tell me.'

'Nope. I've got nothing.'

'Nora,' Sephy said with a warning note of exasperation.

She huffed out a breath. 'He's angry because he had to go back to his job before he'd "saved" me. He probably feels as if he's left something undone and he's annoyed.'

'What a load of crap. Why does he think you need saving? And who from—yourself?'

'Exactly.' She was glad someone was on her side.

'I mean it isn't as if anyone has been worried about you. It isn't as if you'd been burying yourself in your work, giving yourself an ulcer, trying to do way too much on your own and walking around with shoes super-glued to your hand.'

Tears fell unchecked in a steady stream down Nora's face. 'I'm going to hang up now.'

'I think he really liked you,' Sephy said gently.

'Not enough to stay, apparently.'

'Did you even ask him?'

Nora drew her knee up onto the chair and balanced her elbow on it so that her hand could twist soothingly into her hair. 'He told me he would have come back for me, but I was too locked into my world.'

'He meant—'

'I know what he meant. I'm not stupid.'

'Just defensive about it, then.'

Nora sighed. 'No one understands. KPC was Dad's legacy and now it's mine. I made a promise to him. I can't let him down. So, yes, sometimes I come off a little too precious and conflicted about it.'

'Nora, Dad had KPC and a wife, three children and a grandchild. Jared has his company and Amanda. Are you seriously telling me you're going to deny yourself all your chances at having more?'

'Maybe they were better at handling it all than me,' she whispered miserably.

'That's ridiculous. Where is this coming from? You don't think

182

you're worthy of more? You're my big sister. You saved KPC from going under because you went and found Jared and put two King heads together to find a solution. You fixed it so that Jared and Dad could resolve all their differences before Dad died. You're managing a large company through a never-ending recession. You own a penthouse apartment that you bought with your own money. You're a role model for my daughter. And you have a shoe collection better than any other woman on the planet.'

Nora felt her heart swell. 'I love you, Sephy.'

'Then please listen to me. I know out of the three of us you were closest to Dad, but don't put him up on too high a pedestal. He was too blinkered at times. You know we all felt the fallout from that. Don't let yourself be like that. Don't let your life become about one thing only. Or get so blinkered that you can't recognise the people who come along and put themselves front and centre of you and offer you an opportunity to have more—to have balance.'

Nora twisted the coil of hair she had a hold of over and over. Someone already had come along, hadn't they? Someone who was a six foot six Adonis with a giant heart called Ethan Love. He'd ridden into her life on his charger and begun it all with a charming 'Actually, that's three words' and…

Oh. What had she done? Forget super-gluing her shoe to her hand, she'd super-glued those blinkers on and well and truly blinded herself to adding Ethan to her life. As usual she'd thought 'all or nothing' and now he'd gone and she had nothing. She couldn't really blame him. What had she risked openly to let him know that she might be thinking about a different three words.

She sniffed into the phone and said, 'I might come and stay with you for a few weeks.'

'We'd love to have you.'

Then, because she was the elder and it was her duty to tease she said, 'Would that be you and Daisy or you and Luke.'

'Well, I can see you're feeling a bit better,' Sephy bristled. 'I guess my work here is done.' There was a small pause and then,

'You going to be okay?'

'Course. I'm a King and my baby sister has just called me all kind of fierce.'

'Promise me you won't spend the evening working. You could always jump in the car and stay tonight.'

'It's okay. I promise not to do any work. Just some thinking.'

'Okay. Love you.'

'Love you too,' Nora murmured putting the phone down and before she could think twice she pulled open her desk drawer and removed her father's letter to her.

With shaking hands, she slid her fingers under the flap to break the seal. Carefully she unfolded the thick piece of paper and gasped as another colourful thin piece of folded paper floated out.

Chapter Thirteen

My Dearest Leonora,

I came across this when I was searching through some boxes in the study the other day. I had forgotten how your mother used to slip artwork and school projects that the three of you had done onto my desk or into my briefcase for me to find.

I realise that as an adult now, you may look at what I've included with this letter and feel completely distanced from it—embarrassed even.

Please don't be.

Nora snatched up the piece of paper that had floated down to the desk and unfolded it.

Oh my God.

She stared through her tears at the heading at the top of the page in bold orange felt-tip.

Nora's Love List.

The dot of the letter 'I' was a flower head. There was a little bee buzzing over the top of it. The list gave her a sudden flashback to choosing which stickers were important enough to grace the page; she could have been ten years old again.

She couldn't believe she was staring down at it. Didn't understand the meaning of it. Of all the things she had expected her father to say to her, writing to her about something she'd written as a child never even figured.

Her gaze sought out her father's handwriting.

Reading your list again gave me a glimpse into who you were when you were ten and I, regretfully, was too consumed with work to take much notice of my three children.

I see from it that even back then you knew what you wanted—who you were and what you needed to make you happy.

I note that KPC isn't on it! What I wouldn't give to ask you when the exact moment that you knew you wanted it came over you. Or would I? I wonder now whether I encouraged you a little too much and you being the good daughter that you always strived to be rose to the challenge, to please me.

If that is the case, can you forgive an arrogant man who was swept away with the thought of a King at the helm for another forty years?

I question if you know how good you've been for my company, Leonora.

Your company now.

Your company to do with what you want and with no recriminations from the grave. I need you to believe that with every bit of that great big heart that beats so fiercely inside you. The same big fierce heart that wrote your Love List.

I made some mistakes in my life that I am ashamed of and it's taken this cancer eating away at me to make me see that. But what words can I give you to help you live your life now?

I want you to believe you can take KPC to the next level.

Whether you are part of that next level is completely your right to choose.

And I do want you to choose, Leonora.

Like you did in your Love List here.

Choose what is right for you and know that I may never have known quite how to show it, but that I always have, and always will, love you either way.

Your father xxx

Nora felt the sob erupt from her throat.

In reading his letter she had found the father she knew again. She wasn't angry with him and all the things he wasn't. She loved him. He was her father. She was angry with him for dying. Angry with herself for feeling it so deeply.

But most of all she was angry that his passing had forced her to realise that she wanted more in life than the company and not ever putting KPC first felt like the cruellest way of betraying him.

She'd been so scared that in order to run KPC effectively she'd have to sacrifice all her relationships because that was what she had seen her father—her mentor—do.

But here he was telling her not to make his mistakes. Telling her he knew he hadn't followed through with his relationships and made them work while he was alive. Not with Jared, and that was why Jared had left, not with Sephy and that was why she'd invested in Ryan and not with her, Nora, when he'd seen her consuming herself with KPC.

Nora felt as if a giant weight had been lifted off her shoulders.

Getting up from the desk, she walked over to the sink and poured herself a drink of ice- cold water. She drank it down with shaky hands before taking a tissue and blowing her nose.

Feeling a little less like a wreck, she went back to the desk, switched on the Tiffany table lamp and picked up her Love List. She'd been ten when she'd written it. Ten years old and filled with zest for life. Shaped by the type of confidence that growing up with money gives you and already looking around her and wanting to have absolutely everything that she thought would make her life the best and most fulfilled. Writing down all the things she loved had seemed to her growing up, ten-year-old self, eminently sensible and the first step to making sure she'd get the future she had thought she wanted!

1. I love school so I'm going to work hard and come out with good grades so I can get a really good job and tell people what to do. Jared tells me what to do all the time and seems to really like it. Also a good job means I'll be able to buy lots of shoes.

2. I love shoes. Nice shoes. Not the brown ones Mummy makes me wear at the moment. As soon as I'm twelve I'm going to campaign to wear more grown-up shoes, then Sephy can wear all my old shoes and see how she likes it. When I'm older I'll have shoes in every colour and have a special cupboard to keep them all in. I'll probably let Sephy borrow some of them because she is my sister and it's not nice to be horrible to your sister.

3. I love London. Our class visited last week and it was a great big grand adventure. Jared says I probably walked past buildings that Daddy owns.

4. I love adventures. I plan to have lots of them when I grow up. One day I'm going to marry someone who loves adventures exactly as much as me.

5. He must have travelled the world so he'll know lots of stuff and be really interesting and have a job that helps people because that will mean he is kind.

6. He must be good with children because I want lots of them.

7. He must laugh a lot because Mummy says when you have lots of children you need to be able to laugh a lot.

8. He must have blond hair because I have black hair and we'll look better in photographs.

9. He must be really tall because I think I'm going to be really tall and then we'll look right together.

10. He must be able to love me for who I am, which is quite a nice person!!!

Good grief!

She'd been a bolshie little thing.

She never had won the campaign to wear more grown-up shoes. Her mother was too good at seeing her coming a mile off. She'd had to wait until she was thirteen to get her first pair of grown-up shoes and, as a result, to this day, still teasingly told her mother it was her fault she'd developed such a bad shoe 'habit'.

She could remember Jared and Sephy teasing her mercilessly when she'd pinned her Love List on her wall and her not really minding because having it all set in her mind was part of her adventure. Years later, though, when she'd first started bringing boyfriends home, meals around the dinner table were a nightmare as she waited for Jared or Sephy to mention something off her famous Love List.

Her father had said the list had given him a glimpse of who she'd been and what she wanted out of life.

As an adult all she saw was that she'd asked for a bloody knight in shining armour.

She felt her eyes bulge as she remembered she'd thought about this list the day she'd met Ethan. She could have forgiven herself for being superficial if he hadn't then set about ticking every item off the list, as though he'd been conjured from it.

Thinking about him made her wonder if he'd made it to the earthquake site.

Ridiculously she felt like switching on the news to check that there hadn't been any activity in the area.

Then her heart plummeted. What if the next place he was sent was back to an area in conflict? What if he decided to rescue someone else and put himself in danger?

So much for wanting a man with a big heart and a thirst for adventure.

Except...

Nora blew out a breath.

She did. She really wanted that.

She wanted Ethan Love.

He said he would have come back for her...

He'd come into her life when she was hardly at her best and yet he'd shared his patience, wisdom, kindness and fun with her.

If he had considered coming back to her when he'd seen her like that, then surely seeing her at her best would be a no-brainer— wouldn't it? She wondered if she could be enough for him.

189

Then remembered Sephy's staunch defence of her.

She went back and re-read her father's letter.

Then re-read her Love List.

Maybe she had lost her sense of adventure for a while there. She chose to forgive herself. Finally understanding that grief was a process that you had to go through and that unfortunately there was never a definite pattern to it; it was individual to the person you were and the connection you had to the person.

Ethan, with his laidback super-sexy smile, his every challenging look and by letting her know it was all right to feel however she was feeling, had started reawakening her thirst for adventure.

She was supposed to choose her life.

Not wait for someone to choose her.

Her life could include whatever she wanted and she'd work hard to make what she wanted fit.

She chose Ethan.

But what if…

She smiled and reached for her phone.

What was the worst-case scenario?

Ethan walked into the school hall adjacent to where the response team's camp was being dismantled, his hands shoved deep into his pockets. He was pleased to see only a handful of families had had to sleep in the echoing room the night before. A table had been set up at the far end of the room and some of his colleagues were working with town hall officials to ensure that the remaining families had somewhere to go.

By his calculations the school would be up and running again within the next two days. A few last-minute things left to do to ensure the community was able to function going forward and then he would be leaving. He was glad he'd got to come back and help with the last few days of the clean-up operation.

The relief when he'd found Pietro safe and well and happily reunited with both parents had been immense.

God, but he was tired, though.

He'd been sleeping, so he couldn't figure that one out.

Clenching his jaw he ordered his thoughts not to stray to a certain someone.

Too late.

Yeah. Okay.

She was the reason.

He still wasn't quite sure how it had all gone so downhill so quickly.

He'd honestly thought that during what had turned out to be their last night together that he'd been showing her with his body—asking her with his body—to give him a chance.

He'd been whistling in that shower the next morning, basking in the knowledge that she'd understand he had to return to finish what he'd been part of, but that afterwards...

Yeah. Complete prize idiot. Because in the event he'd had his answer before apparently needing to ask the question.

His ego thanked her.

But his heart felt like it had taken a good kicking.

There he'd been making love to her. Making plans.

There she'd been saying goodbye. Saying no thank you.

When he'd come out of the bathroom and seen her dressing, it still hadn't registered but then he'd seen her face. He'd realised she must have seen that report on his laptop and balked.

It had been obvious in the way she'd shut down.

She'd judged him and sentenced him when there was no way she could have had time to read it in its entirety.

Who needed someone like that in their life anyway?

No need to make a fool of himself and plead his case.

Beg.

Okay, so he should have told her about the report and about the fact that he'd been sent home. Couldn't he be forgiven for putting off not wanting her to think badly of him when he had already been doing a superb job of feeling badly about himself as it was?

It wasn't like he wasn't going to tell her ever. He'd been planning on talking to her about it over the meal they'd had but he'd got so distracted by her.

Then she'd read it and thought badly of him. She'd made it clear. They'd had their fun. She couldn't risk more. Not with him. Not with someone who was potentially reckless. Not with someone she was convinced wanted to fix the world—fix her, when—damn it—didn't he like her as she was?

Love her as she was?

He'd had that gem pointed out to him by his brother, of all people.

And now his heart was a disaster zone.

He left the school hall to head back to the camp and help dismantle the last of the tents.

The sun was setting low in the sky. A fiery yellow-orange globe in a blanket of dusky pink and he wanted automatically to share it with Nora. He fished his phone out and took a picture, tempted to send it to her. With what, though? A 'Wish You Were Here' tag?

He smoothed his hair back and stared down at the picture he'd taken.

It had only been a week since she'd shot out of his hotel room like a pack of demons were on her tail, but there hadn't been one moment of that week that he hadn't missed her.

Missed the stubborn lift of her chin.

Missed the little 'v' she got in her forehead when she was working through a problem or ramping up to get all angry at him for teasing her.

Missed her beautiful soft smile when she woke up in the morning and her eyes locked straight on to him.

It wasn't only that he missed her. As more days went by he'd had to finally admit that he was looking at a severe case of more of an ego and less of the hero in the way he'd reacted to her saying goodbye.

He should have gone ahead and asked her for that chance. He

should have argued, out-talked or, hell, he should have kissed her into agreeing they deserved a shot at being together.

As he stood with the setting sun behind him, the remains of the camp in front of him, all he could think about was walking back into KPC offices and demanding she listen to him.

Insist that what they had was more than simple fun.

That, in fact, maybe it was everything…

He heard the motorbike before he saw it.

It's rumbling engine thundered closer and briefly he thought that getting around the area on two wheels was much more sensible than trying to navigate some of the more broken-up roads in a car.

He turned his head towards the sound, squinting as the reflection from the setting sun bounced off chrome handlebars.

The bike came to a stop a few feet in front of him.

The rider shut off the engine and flicked the bike stand down.

The next thing Ethan knew, the rider was gracefully dismounting, reminding him of… his mouth went dry.

The rider withdrew their helmet and shook out glorious, layered, shiny black hair.

Hair he'd fisted in his hands.

Hair he'd tucked behind her ears.

Ethan took a step towards the vision in front of him. 'Jesus.'

'Well, Nora, anyway,' quipped the voice. 'Hello, Ethan.'

Her smile was soft.

Beautiful.

Hesitant.

'What the hell are you doing here,' he rushed out to cover the sound of his heart thumping. *Real suave, Ethan.*

Nora fiddled with the strap of her helmet, fluffed her hair around her shoulders, opened her mouth to speak and then closed it again. Finally she put the helmet on the bike seat, gestured helplessly with her hands and then said, 'So, I was owed some holiday.'

Ethan folded his arms to stop himself reaching out for her. 'Is that right? Well, you are the boss.'

Nora's smile grew more certain. 'Yes. Yes, I am.'

'What about the Moorfield account,' he asked stupidly instead of asking why she was standing in front of him.

'Turns out I have some pretty damn good project managers who work for me. Not to mention a personal assistant only too happy to step up and hold the fort for a while.'

'Great. *Why* are you here?'

She shrugged her shoulders nonchalantly. 'I had a taste for adventure.'

'Damn it, Nora,' How could she be so laissez-faire. 'This place isn't about adventure. For one thing it's still dangerous. But, most importantly, there are people here who have lost everything, who are trying to piece their lives back together again. The last thing they need is someone looking around in fascination.'

'I know that, Ethan,' she chided, all trace of teasing gone.

'Do you? Because I won't let you come in here and—' he broke off as her tone and the look in his eyes registered. He was the first person to react to being judged unfairly and here he was subjecting her to it. His hand lifted to run over the back of his head in an attempt to gather his thoughts. Her riding up on that motorbike of hers had scattered any cool-factor he'd ever had about him to the wind. 'I'm sorry. I realise you wouldn't come here with the intention of doing that.'

'I'm glad you know me well enough to know that, Ethan.' She gave him a long look as if she was drinking him in, fixing the moment in her mind and he knew he was standing before her with the same determination to record every detail of her. After a while she dragged her gaze to the left to take in what was left of their camp. With a jerk of her head she said, 'Feel like showing me around your world?'

The grin began at the far corners of his mouth. 'I feel like doing "something" right now—I'm not sure a tour is it.'

Nora's smile grew at an equal rate. 'What do you feel like doing, then?'

Oh, he was definitely about to show her. He raised his fingers and beckoned her closer. 'Come here,' he ordered softly.

She raised an eyebrow at him, but then started walking slowly towards him.

Two steps in and he closed the distance, wrapped her up in his arms, lifted her feet clear off the floor and lowered his mouth to hers.

God, he'd missed this most of all, he thought as his lips rubbed over hers and she opened her mouth for him and fire lit his blood. He felt her hands climb over his shoulders to cling and he loved it and pulled her into his arms even tighter.

Now that he was holding her he didn't think he could let her go. There was never the slightest misunderstanding between them when they were communicating in this way. But gradually he realised where they were and that he couldn't walk off with her into the sunset and straight into the nearest hotel.

If he wanted that chance with her then they needed to talk and listen and plan. He squeezed her harder to him because crazy, wonderful Leonora King hadn't swapped stilettos and business suits for biker boots and leathers and come all this way for nothing. She'd come for him. That was why she was here, wasn't it? He hadn't got that wrong, had he?

Reluctantly lowering her feet back to the floor, he rubbed his lips against hers once, twice more and then broke the kiss to rest his forehead against hers.

His fingers stroked her hair back behind her ears and his eyes searched hers as he tried to calm his breathing.

'Come on,' he said stepping to the side and taking her hand in his, 'let's go for a walk down to the olive grove. It's not far and we can talk while we walk.' He felt Nora's hand squeeze in agreement against his and as they walked down the road he searched his head for a way to start. 'I hear Ryan has made contact with Sephy,' he told her.

'He did,' she confirmed. 'Sephy's meeting up with him next

week.'

'And how do you feel about that?'

'A little over-protective still.' He felt her look at him and smile. 'I am impressed with what he's done to turn his life around, though.'

'So am I,' Ethan admitted. 'When I've been talking to him, it's a different Ryan to the one I used to know, years ago. He has a very good sense of where he went wrong and what he needs to keep doing to stay on the right path.' Not to mention an opinion on what I should have done to fight for you, he thought with a wry smile. Again his gaze flicked down to her as if to check she really was walking by his side, her hand in his. 'Sephy's going to find him quite changed.'

'She'll handle it. To be honest it actually helps he's moving to Heathstead with his girlfriend. He'll have support and won't be relying on Sephy, which I think she'd find awkward. Anyway, she must be okay about it all because she's already told Mum what's happening.'

'How is your mum?'

'Good, I think. She's staying out in New York until Jared and Amanda's wedding now.'

He watched as Nora lifted her head to gaze out through the lines of olive trees and survey the land. 'Is she still thinking of selling the estate?'

'I wouldn't be surprised. She hasn't said anything more to me about it, but,' Nora stopped and shrugged her shoulders, 'if she does it'll because it's the right thing for her.'

'You'll miss the place, though,' he said gently.

'I will, but,' she looked at him from under her lashes, 'somehow it doesn't seem as big a deal as I first thought. Maybe that's because I've been reminded that a house or a business isn't the only thing you can give your heart to.'

Ethan's heart did a little flexing in his chest. He really wanted to kiss her again. Here amongst the olive trees, with the sun setting behind her, but he hadn't talked to her about everything yet.

Nora looked up at him, her chin tilting up to challenge, 'Ethan?'

'Yes, Leonora?'

'It's great catching each other up about everyone in our lives, but do you think we'll get around to talking about us anytime soon? Just, you know, so that I can get my nerve to hold out a little longer.'

He smiled and praying that she wouldn't think too badly of him, he said, 'I need to talk to you about that report first,' and with a gentle skim of his finger down her forehead to chase away the tine 'v' of confusion, he began telling her about breaking protocol to go into the building alone to get Pietro out.

'But I never saw that report,' she said when he had finished.

'I'd left my laptop charging before we'd gone out. I was convinced you had seen it and didn't want to saddle yourself with someone who could put people in danger like that.'

'Ethan,' Nora chastised. 'You would never be reckless. You're trained and experienced in what you do. Don't you think they'd have weeded you out years ago if they thought you had a reckless streak or that you could endanger your team or the people you were helping? You would have assessed the situation automatically when you heard Pietro call out and you would have carried on assessing the situation the closer you got to him. The only error of judgement you made was in not telling anyone. If you had, or if there had been others around to help you, you would have all been caught in the aftershock.'

'That's pretty much what the report concluded,' he told her sheepishly.

'Exactly. Reckless, my eye.'

Ethan burst out laughing. It was a pretty powerful feeling to have her on his side. It was why it had hurt so much when he'd thought she wasn't.

She'd never judged him badly. That was his own thing that he carried around from place to place. And something he was going to try and leave behind.

He had a feeling it would be much easier with Nora championing him.

'I shouldn't have let you walk out of my hotel room like that,' he told her gently.

'I shouldn't have let me walk out your hotel room like that,' she answered back. 'I thought you were saying goodbye to me that night and the next morning I just wanted to be gone. I was a coward. Then, when you told me you would have come back for me if I'd asked you to stay, all I could think was that I'd screwed everything up with you and the only reason you would want to be with me was because I needed fixing. I was afraid you thought your job was only to be my knight in shining armour.'

'Nora King, the one thing you will never be is a coward and I'm sorry that my stupidly overlarge ego ever made you think I thought you needed saving or fixing, for real. Because you don't. You are more than fine just the way you are. I tried to show you that in other ways but maybe I didn't succeed. You were grieving. You never needed a knight in shining armour, Nora.'

'No, I didn't. What I needed was someone to remind me of that. And you did. I already knew I was a little lost. You dragged me out of my panic at every turn. When I first met you all I could think was "Nooo, don't do this to me, world, I don't have room for you on my To Do list".'

'Yeah?' Ethan swung her round to face him. 'When I saw you strut out of your office in those killer heels of yours, all I could think was that I definitely wanted to put you on my "To Do" list.'

Nora laughed and rolled her eyes before sobering and reaching out to place her hand against Ethan's cheek. 'So, I'm thinking... what if we fell in love with each other?' she whispered.

'What if we did?' he whispered back.

'I'm thinking that wouldn't be a worst-case scenario. I'm thinking that would be...fine.'

Ethan took the hand that was resting against his face and placed a kiss into the centre of its palm. Staring down at her he smiled and said, 'I fell a little in love with you the moment I saw you trying so hard to work out a way to make your meeting when you had a shoe super-glued to your hand. All that passion lurking in the depths of your gorgeous chocolate-brown eyes,' he shook his head slightly in wonder. 'And I fell all the way in love with you when you didn't back off from trying to help me work out why I couldn't sleep. When you didn't get spooked, or assume you knew what it felt like—you simply listened and without judgement, let me see for myself.'

Nora smiled up at him, her heart shining out of her eyes for him to see. 'I fell a little in love with you when you told me you wanted to help me out of family loyalty. Of course it helped tremendously that you looked exactly like what I'd stated in my Love List.'

'Your what?'

Nora grinned harder. 'I'll explain later. I fell a little bit more in love with you when you told me for the thousandth time that it was okay to still be grieving and you didn't seem fazed at all by it—as if you knew it was separate from who I was. I fell *all* the way in love with you when I saw you teaching Daisy how to perfect her wellie-wanging aim and you were so good with her and I thought that is what I want. The "more" that I wanted was you.'

Ethan bent his head and kissed her softly on the lips.

'It's getting dark,' Nora said, opening her eyes and gazing around.

'Let's start walking back. I should tell you that being stuck in that building with Pietro I made some decisions. I plan on focusing a little more on fundraising, being sent on deployment less. I wanted the report to clear me so that I could leave it behind on the best terms. I want to be more involved in Love Leisure. Seeing all your passion for KPC made me realise I can combine both jobs and still devote more time to building up the business. Maybe move HQ from Hull into London.'

'Won't you miss this? You're so good at it and it's part of who you are. I wouldn't ever want you to think you had to stop for me.'

'I'll still go out sometimes,' Ethan said, coming to a stop in front of Nora's motorbike. 'But it'll be different now. I won't want to be away so much. I've found my permanent home now—you. I love you, Nora King.'

'I love you, Ethan Love. Oh, and I have a present for you,' Nora said, skipping joyfully over to the bike and removing a box from one of the panniers. She passed it to him and nodded that he should go ahead and open it. 'Well, actually it's more a present for me,' she declared.

Ethan opened the box and laughed as he withdrew one definitely-in-need-of-breaking-in, brown leather work boot, by its shoelace.

Nora withdrew the matching boot by its shoelace too. 'I figured I might want to come with you sometimes, because you're my home too. And well, a girl's gotta have the right shoes for the occasion, right?'

Ethan laughed and wrapped her back up in his arms, the boot dangling from his hand.

'You are obsessed,' he claimed.

Nora hugged him to her, the other boot dangling down his back from where she clutched the lace, tightly. 'Obsessed and in love,' she replied with a happy sigh. She thought about her Love List and grinned. She was hugging everything it represented and more.

Ethan and she were each other's futures.

Whatever they ended up doing about their respective jobs, she knew that they would discuss it together and make the decision that was right for them as a couple because in each other they had both found their "more", their futures, their home.